U0145457

實踐大學應用外語學系專任副教授

李普生 著

即選即用 商務英文成語 慣用語

五南圖書出版公司 印行

前言 (Preface)

在說明本書編輯的宗旨和方法之前，我們要先花點時間來了解究竟慣用語、成語、或諺語究竟是什麼？

何謂慣用語(idioms)或成語(phrases)？

所謂的慣用語及成語就是一連串單字的組合，而它所表達的意思又和各個單字字義的總和有所不同的用語。慣用語及成語可能在某種情境下有它一定的字面解釋，但在其他種狀況中卻又意有所指。另外一個讓慣用語和成語難懂甚至於不好用的因素是它們很少會遵循字義或文法的規定和要求。舉例說：

「To sit on the fence」可以依字面直譯為「坐在籬笆或圍牆上」，如：

I sat on the fence and watched the game. 我坐在圍牆上看球賽。

但它真正的意思是「某人對某事無法做出明確的決定。」

所以：

◉ The politician sat on the fence and would not give his opinion about the tax issue.

這位政治人物對賦稅一事立場曖昧且不願表示個人看法。

雖然語言不同，但在類似狀況下，來自不同文化背景的人都能用自己的方式表達類似的用法。想要了解這些用語不難，但有些慣用語和成語則因緣起於古早習俗傳統再加上時日變遷而無法用常理來判斷，這些原因也往往會造成認知上的差異甚至於誤解。例如：

　　「To hold one's horse」（耐心等待某人或某事）若直接依字面解讀，下面的這句話還真是讓聽者丈二金剛摸不著頭腦：

◉ "Hold your horses," I said when my friend started to leave the store.

　　更有些慣用語和成語更會因為緣起於英語系國家中一些日常習俗或活動及運動，對於來自他國的語言學者而言，真不啻是鴨子聽雷，有聽沒懂！例如：

　　「To cover all of one's bases」（充分準備以應付某個狀況）：這個慣用法實際是來自美國人的全民運動棒球，在一場棒球比賽中，所有球員都必須講個個壘包防守好。所以：

◉ I tried to cover all my bases when I went to the job interview.
　　當我去面試時，我試著能面面俱到。

慣用語和成語是如何組合而成的？

　　大部分的慣用語和成語都有它們的獨特且固定的規定，如：「to sit on the fence」絕不會說成「to sit on a fence」或「to sit on fences」，而「on top of」（掌握）也絕不能說成「on the top of...」（在…之上）。儘管擅自更動慣用用語或成語的組合規定會被認為錯誤，但有些更動反倒營造出新的用語和意義。例如：

「To be broken」（打破），如在：

◉ The lamp is broken so I cannot easily read my book.
　　檯燈破了，所以我無法輕易地去看書。

但，

◉ I am broke and I cannot go to a movie tonight.
　　我破產了，所以今晚我無法去看電影。

當然，改變的形式很多，而每種改變都會使原本的用語變得更生動：

- I sat on the fence and did not give my opinion.
- Many people are sitting on the fence and not want to give their opinions.
- The politician has been sitting squarely in the middle of the fence since the election. 自從選舉後，這位政治人物就一直保持中立。

上述就是為何有時在字典中想要在字典中找出某句慣用語的意思並不是件容易事的原因。

何謂短語動詞(phrasal verb)？

所謂的短語動詞就是以「動詞+副詞」、「動詞+介系詞」、以及「動詞+副詞+介系詞」所組成的動詞。因為從它組成的每個字的字義，通常可以很容易的就找到它的字面意；但通常是它有「弦外之音」或「意有所指」因而使得短語動詞難以馴服。例如：

1 動詞 + 副詞 (run + around)

- The dog ran around the fire hydrant. 狗繞著消防栓跑。
- I spent the day running around downtown.

  我花了整天的時間在城裡東奔西跑。

2 動詞 + 介系詞 (run + into)

◉ The car ran into the truck on the busy street.

這部車在忙碌的街上撞上了一部卡車。

◉ I ran into my friend in a restaurant yesterday.

我昨天在餐廳裡碰到我朋友。

3 動詞 + 副詞 + 介系詞 (run +along/ around + with)

◉ The dog is running along with the bicycle.

這狗追著腳踏車跑。

◉ The boy is running around with a bad group of people.

這男孩和一群壞人做朋友。

有些慣用語除了短語動詞外還加上一些其他的字，而這些另加的字通常位置固定且決定這個慣用語或成語的真正意思。例如：

「to run (verb) around (adverb) like a chicken with its head cut off」（無頭蒼蠅）：

◉ I ran around like a chicken with its head cut off as I tried to prepare for my holidays. 我像無頭蒼蠅般地在忙著準備過節。

諺語(Proverb)

　　除了慣用語和成語外，還有諺語。何謂諺語？諺語就是許多人都能朗朗上口的說法或句子。這些「老生常談」往往是智慧的結晶、歷久不變的事實、或是寓意深邃的經驗或體驗。諺語在所有語言中都能找到，而諺語除了每每具有規範約束而且是人人都該「起而效之」的魔力外，更會使語言文字生動。例如：

「money does not grow on trees」（錢又不是從天上掉下來的）：

◉ The girl's father often says that money does not grow on trees when she asks him for money.

　　當那女孩向她父親要錢時，他總是說錢又不是從天上掉下來的。

「the early bird catches the worm」（先到先贏）：

◉ My boss always comes to work early because he believes that the early bird catches the worm.

　　因為我老闆相信先到先贏，所以他每天總是很早就來上班。

「The pen is mightier than the sword」（文字勝過蠻力）：

- The pen is mightier than the sword and a good idea or strong beliefs will defeat the strongest army.

文字勝過蠻力，好的理念和強烈的信仰會打敗最強的軍隊。

本書之所以訂名為「即選即用商務英文成語慣用語」的原因是因為現今在各行各業中，每兩個工作中就有一個和服務業有關。既是服務，那人與人之間的溝通交流勢必在所難免，也正因此，如何有效（效果+效率）且又能生動活潑言簡意賅就成為口語表達中不可或缺的技巧。就好像我們在說中文時，或在正式場合中引經據典或在輕鬆閒談時用草根味十足的俚語一樣，我們在使用英文時，也會希望對方能明確地得到訊息但又不會讓彼此溝通太過嚴謹，若能適時地利用些歐美文化中家喻戶曉的說法來拉近彼此的距離；達到目的且多交個朋友，何樂不為？

本書所收錄的成語諺語和慣用語依性質可分成四個單元：「一般職場運作」，「談判協商交涉」，「金錢相關」，「數字遊戲」，「五顏六色」，「民以食為天」，以及「佛要金裝人要衣裝」。所有列舉的詞句都依英文字母順序編排，中英解釋再佐以例句來說明用法。雖冠上商務英文且使用在職場表達，但實際使用則無須過於拘謹在一定要和商場運作有關的情境中才行；所謂的「萬變不離其宗」，本書中所提供的表達該是「放之四海皆準」的工具。只要是用英語英文做工具的場合，適時地亮出一句話，一定會讓與你對談的外國友人刮目相看！就算是準備多益、雅思或托福考試或單純賦閒

在家自修的人，本書中所舉出的詞句也會讓您趕到實用有趣和刺激。

　　多看例句，多大聲朗讀，多放手去嘗試；只有不斷地練習和使用才能確實掌握這些乍看下似乎難懂但一旦掌握後又趣味無窮的成語諺語和慣用語。希望大家都能成為真箇「職場表達一級棒」！

目錄 (Contents)

Business Idioms
一般商業片語

一般商業片語 (Business Idioms)

across the board：including everyone or everything 全面，通盤，所有

> The computer company decided to give the workers an **across-the-board** increase in their salary.
>
> 這家電腦公司決定給員工全面性的加薪。

adjourn a meeting：to end a meeting 休會

> We **adjourned the meeting** for lunch; we will resume it at two in the afternoon.
>
> 我們因午餐而休會，下午兩點再開始。

at a loss：at less than the cost, at a financial loss 賠錢，虧損

> The store was selling things **at a loss** so the prices were very low.
>
> 因商店賠錢賣商品所以價格很低。

bail a company out/bail out a company：to rescue a company that has financial problems 紓困

> The government **bailed out the bank** to maintain stability in the economy.
>
> 政府為了維持經濟穩定而對銀行提供紓困。

ball park figure [estimate]：a rough estimate or figure 概估，大約數字

> The contractor gave us a **ball park figure** for the cost of repairing the new building.
>
> 承包商對整修建築物費用向我們提出概估。

一般商業片語 (Business Idioms)

- **bang for the buck**：value for the money 物超所值；賺到了

  We were able to get much **bang for the buck** when we advertised on the Internet.

  在網路上打廣告讓我們賺到了。

- **banker's hours**：short work hours 短工時

  My friend owns his own business and works **banker's hours** most days.

  我的朋友自擁有自己的事業，所以他大部分的工作時間都很短。

- **bankroll someone**：to supply someone with money, to finance someone 資助

  The movie actor **bankrolled his son** while his son was producing his first movie.

  這位電影明星在他兒子製作他第一部影片時資助他。

- **bean counter**：an accountant 會計

  We asked the **bean counter** to look at the figures in the new budget.

  我們要求會計去看看我們預算中的數字。

- **big cheese [gun, wheel]**：an important person, a leader 大人物，領導人

  The new director was a **big wheel** in his previous company.

  新主管在他以前的公司是個大人物。

一般商業片語 (Business Idioms)

bigwig：an important person, a leader 大人物，領導者

> Some of the **bigwigs** of our company came to visit our factory.
>
> 公司的一些大人物來工廠訪視。

bottom drops [falls out of] something：a collapse occurs and prices fall below an earlier low price 價格跌破谷底

> When the **bottom fell out of** the coffee market, many coffee producers had to stop doing business.
>
> 當咖啡市場跌落谷底時很多咖啡生產商必須休業。

bottom line：the total, the final figure on a balance sheet, the results (of a business) 帳本底線，盈虧結算線；最重要的事，重點

> After we examined the **bottom line** of the company, we decided not to invest in it.
>
> 在調查過這家公司的虧損後，我們決定不在它身上做投資。
>
> As an office worker, the **bottom line** is to do everything to the best of one's ability.
>
> 身為公司員工，最重要的是要事事全力以赴。

bottom out：to reach the lowest or worst point 在最低處

> The value of my stock has begun to **bottom out** and it should soon begin to increase in value.
>
> 我的股票已到最低價位，它應該很快就會開始上漲。

一般商業片語 (Business Idioms)

- **bounce a check**：to write a check in which you do not have enough money in your bank account 跳票

  > The young man **bounced a check** when he tried to pay his rent.
  >
  > 這年輕人在付房租時開的支票跳票了。

- **boys in the kitchen**：a close circle of people, usually decision-making level of managerial personnel, with the power and authority needed to change the course of operation without getting others' consent or approval 幕後黑手，私底下運作的人，知道內情的人

  > The **boys in the kitchen** told us that the factory will be closed next year.
  >
  > 了解內情的人告訴我們工廠明年將關門。

- **break even**：to have expenses equal profits 收支平衡，打平

  > After three months the company was able to **break even** and begin to make a profit.
  >
  > 三個月後公司打平且開始有利潤。

- **budget crunch [squeeze]**：a situation where there is not enough money in the budget 預算不足

  > There is a severe **budget squeeze** at our company.
  >
  > 我們公司有嚴重的預算不足。

B

一般商業片語 (Business Idioms)

- **buy a stake in (something)**：to buy part ownership of a company or other enterprise 購買部分主權

  The large bank is planning to **buy a stake in** the small trading company.
  這家大銀行正在計畫購買這家小證券公司的部分主權。

- **buy off (someone)/buy (someone) off**：to use a gift or money to divert someone from their duty (similar to a bribe and something illegal) 收買賄賂

  The land developer tried to **buy off** the politician but he was not successful.
  土地開發商想要收買政治人物但沒成功。

- **buy out (someone/something)/buy (someone/something) out**：to buy the ownership or the majority share of something 收購

  The large company decided to **buy out** the small textile company.
  這家大公司決定收購小紡織公司。

- **buy (something) on credit**：to buy something without paying cash 賒帳買

  My friend had no money so he decided to **buy** some furniture **on credit**.
  我朋友沒錢所以他用記帳的方法買了些家具。

- **by a long shot**：by a big difference 壓倒性地；相差甚遠地

  Our company beat out the bids of other companies **by a long shot**.
  我們公司在競標中壓倒性地打敗其他公司。

一般商業片語 (Business Idioms)

- **a calculated risk**：an action that may fail but has a good chance to succeed 計畫中的風險；一件事雖有失敗的可能但成功的率相當高

  > The company took **a calculated risk** when they put the new computer on the market.
  >
  > 公司在上市新電腦時已知道有失敗的可能。

- **call a meeting in order**：to start a meeting 開始會議

  > Our supervisor **called the meeting in order** after everyone arrived.
  >
  > 我們的主管在所有人到達後宣布開會。

- **captain of industry**：a top corporation officer 同業中的領導者

  > The president of our company was a **captain of industry** and when he retired he was appointed to many government boards.
  >
  > 我們公司的總裁是同業中的領導者。當他退休後，他被指定參加許多政府的委員會。

- **carry a motion**：to support or win acceptance for a motion or proposal or idea in a meeting 使提案通過

  > I was able to **carry a motion** at last night's meeting.
  >
  > 我在昨晚的會議中設法讓我的議案通過。

- **carry over (something)/carry (something) over**：to transfer a figure or number or cost from one column or time to another 將數字轉記到…，結轉；遺留；延後

  > Our company will **carry over** last year's losses to this year.
  >
  > 我們公司將會把去年的損失計入今年的帳目中。

一般商業片語 (Business Idioms)

- **carry the day**：to win complete support 贏得全體的支持

  The manager's idea **carried the day** and everyone supported him with enthusiasm.

  經理的點子得到所有人熱情的同意和支持。

- **carry through with (something)**：to put something into action, to do something 執行

  The steel company will **carry through with** their plan to restructure operations.

  鋼鐵公司將依計畫執行營運重整。

- **circulate the agenda**：to distribute a list of other information about what will be discussed in a meeting 傳閱議程

  We **circulated the agenda** for the meeting last week.

  我們上星期已傳閱了會議議程。

- **close out (something)/close (something) out**：to sell the whole or all of something 出清

  The company decided to **close out** the store and sell the remaining stock very cheap.

  公司決定關閉商店並將存貨廉價清空。

- **close the book**：to stop taking order, to end the bookkeeping period 截止（收訂單）；結帳

  The company will **close the book** at the end of December.

  公司將在十二月結帳。

一般商業片語 (Business Idioms)

come down in price：to lower the price of one's product; to become cheaper 削價

We were forced to **come down in price** in order to sell our target number of cars for the month.

我們被迫削價以便達到本月的預定銷售汽車數量。

come on strong：to overwhelm others with very strong language or personality 來勢洶洶

The salesman **came on strong** at the meeting and angered the other members of the team.

這名業務員在會議中來勢洶洶並因此而激怒了其他小組成員。

company man：a person who always works hard for his company and supports the company policies 公司人

My father was a **company man** and he always put in extra effort for his company.

我的父親是個公司人而他也總是為公司做額外的付出。

company town：a town dominated by one industry or company 公司城（因某公司所在而興起的城市）

The **company town** faced severe economic times when the coal mine closed.

公司城在煤礦關閉後面臨嚴重的經濟問題。

crunch numbers：to do mathematical calculations 計算

The account loves to **crunch numbers** and he is one of the top managers in our company.

這名會計喜愛計算數字而他也是公司裡數一數二的經理之一。

一般商業片語 (Business Idioms)

cut a deal：to make a business arrangement or contact with someone 成交

> I was able to **cut a deal** with the contractor and we paid very little for our new kitchen.
>
> 我和包商達成交易並為我們的新廚房付出了很少的錢。

cut back：to use fewer or less of something 縮減，減少

> The company has been **cutting back** on entertainment expenses recently.
>
> 公司最近減少在交際上的花費。

cut corners：to economize, to try to spend less money 節省時間、精神或精力；走近路，投機

> We have been forced to **cut corners** on expenses during these severer economic times.
>
> 在這些經濟不景氣的時期我們被迫在花費上動手腳。
>
> It might be a good idea to **cut corners** through the park if we want to get there on time.
>
> 穿過公園走近路也許是準時到達那裡的好辦法。
>
> Instead of **cutting corners** in elevating oneself intellectually, Jack decided to become a late-bloomer.
>
> 與其在自我智能提升上投機取巧，傑克決定當個大器晚成的人。

一般商業片語 (Business Idioms)

- **cut off (someone/something)/ cut (someone/something) off**：to interrupt or stop someone or something 中斷；切斷

  The speech by our manager was **cut off** when the electricity went off in the building.
  經理的演講因為建築物內電力中斷而停止。

- **cut one's losses**：to do something in order to stop losing additional money or time etc. 減少（時間金錢）的損失

  We should sell the old machinery soon and try to **cut our losses**.
  我們應趕緊把舊機器賣掉並試著減少損失。

- **defeat a motion**：to defeat an idea or proposal in a meeting 封殺提案

  We easily **defeated the motion** to change the dates for next year's convention.
  我們輕鬆的封殺了改變明年大會日期的議案。

- **deliver the goods**：to succeed in doing a good job of something 順利達成目標

  The new manager is not very popular but he is able to **deliver the goods**.
  新經理不受人歡迎但他能達成目標。

- **double check (something)**：to check something again to confirm that it is correct 確認

  We must **double check** the new product prices before the price list is printed.
  在印製價格表前我們一定要再三確認產品價格。

一般商業片語 (Business Idioms)

- **draw up a contract**：to make or draft a contract 起草合約

  The lawyer spent several hours **drawing up a new contract**.

  律師花了幾個小時起草新合約。

- **face value (of something)**：the worth or price printed on a stamp, bond, note, piece of paper money etc.; the seeming worth or truth of something 表面價值；面值

  Although the **face value** of the postage stamp was very low, it sold at auction for much money.

  儘管郵票的面值很低但在拍賣會上售價卻很高。

- **fair play**：equal and correct action toward someone; justice 公平的比賽，光明正大的行為

  The company has a reputation for **fair play** when they are bargaining with their employees.

  這家公司在和員工交涉時一向以正大光明著稱。

- **figure out (something)/ figure (something) out**：to find an answer by thinking about something 想出，弄清楚

  Everyone is trying to **figure out** what our boss is going to do with the new equipment.

  所有人都在試著想出老闆將如何處置新機器。

- **float (someone) a loan**：to loan somebody a loan 貸款

  I asked the bank to **float a loan** so that I could buy a new car.

  我向銀行貸款以便我能買部新車。

F

一般商業片語 (Business Idioms)

gain ground：to go forward, to make progress 有進展

Our company is **gaining ground** in its attempt to be the best in the industry.

我們公司在變成同行間第一的努力上有了進展。

get a break：to get an opportunity or good deal 好運；有機會；鬆口氣

We were able to **get a break** on the price of the paint and we saved much money.

我們能在油漆價格上鬆口氣並省了許多錢。

get a raise：to get an increase in one's salary 加薪

My sister works hard and she recently **got a raise** in her new job.

我的姊姊工作努力而且她剛在新工作上加薪。

get off the ground：to make a successful beginning 成功的起步

We were unable to **get** the new product **off the ground** but we will try again next year.

我們無法讓新產品順利起步但明年我們會再試一次。

give (someone) the green light：to give someone the permission or approval to do something 同意某人做某事

Our boss **gave us the green light** to begin work on the new sales campaign.

我們老闆同意我們開始新促銷活動的工作。

G

一般商業片語 (Business Idioms)

- **go belly up**：to go out of business because of financial problem 肚皮翻上來；倒閉

  The small computer company **went belly up** several months ago.

  這間小電腦公司幾個月前倒閉了。

- **go over the books**：to check and analyze the accounting records of a company 查帳

  We hired an outside accountant to **go over** our **books**.

  我們僱用了位外面的會計來查帳。

- **go public**：to become a public company and to sell the company stock to the public 公開上市

  The stock of the Internet company rose very quickly after the company **went public**.

  網路公司的股票價格在上市後上漲得很快。

- **hang out one's shingle**：to open one's own business (usually as a professional in some field)（在某個專業領域中）掛牌自行開業

  My friend decided to **hang out his shingle** as a dentist soon after he finished school.

  我朋友在學校畢業後立即決定自行開業成為牙醫。

- **a hard sell**：a way of selling something that is very aggressive and using much pressure 強力推銷

  The car salesman gave us **a hard sell** so we went to another car dealer.

  汽車推銷員強力推銷所以我們決定到另一家汽車經銷商處。

一般商業片語 (Business Idioms)

have a stake in (something)：to have part ownership of a company or other business 因擁有部分所有權而有利害關係

> The large oil company **has a stake in** the new oil exploration company.
> 這家大石油公司擁有新的石油探勘公司的部分股份。

have one's finger in the pie：to be involved in something, to receive money for something 涉案，收取賄賂

> The new manager **has his finger in the pie** of many small businesses.
> 新經理收取許多小事業體的賄賂。

have the floor：to have permission to speak in a meeting 有發言權

> The president **had the floor** for almost an hour during the meeting.
> 董事長在會議中說了將近一個小時的話。

heads will roll：someone will pay for the consequence; someone is going to have a hard time 人頭落地；有人要倒楣

> **Heads will roll** when our boss learns about the money that we have lost.
> 老闆知道我們損失了多少錢後有人會倒楣。

hold a meeting：to conduct a meeting 舉行會議

> We plan to **hold a meeting** next week to discuss the problems with our new product.
> 我們下星期舉行會議來討論新產品的問題。

一般商業片語 (Business Idioms)

in black and white：in writing 白紙黑字寫出來

> The company refused to deal with the customer's complaints until they were **in black and white**.
>
> 公司拒絕處理客戶的不滿除非他們以書面的方式表達。

in charge of (someone/something)：to be in control of someone or something, to be responsible for someone or something 負責某人或某事

> My sister has been **in charge of** buying supplies at her company for many years.
>
> 我姊妹多年來都負責她公司的文具採購。

in short supply：not enough of something, less than the amount or number needed 短缺，不足

> Experienced computer programmers are **in short supply** in our company.
>
> 我們公司缺有經驗的電腦程式設計員。

in stock：available or ready to sell or use 庫存

> The store does not have any printer **in stock**.
>
> 商店內沒有印表機的庫存。

in the black：to be successful, to be making money, to be profitable 有盈餘利潤

> The new company has been **in the black** for many years.
>
> 新公司許多年來都有利潤盈餘。

一般商業片語 (Business Idioms)

- **in the long run**：over a long period of time 到後來，長久

  > The company has been losing money but **in the long run** they should make a profit.
  >
  > 公司一直賠錢但到最後應該會有利潤。

- **in the loop**：part of a group of people that is kept up-to-date with information about something 了解知曉內情的集團

  > I began to work in the evening and I was no longer **in the loop** at our company.
  >
  > 我開始上晚班所以我已經不再是了解公司內情的人了。

- **in the market for (something)**：to be ready to buy something, to want to buy something 想買…

  > We are **in the market for** a new computer.
  >
  > 我們想買一部新電腦。

- **in the red**：to be losing money, to be unprofitable 赤字；虧損

  > The company has been **in the red** since the price of oil began to rise rapidly.
  >
  > 公司從油價急速上漲後就一直虧損。

- **in the works**：to be in preparation, to be in the process of being planned or developed 建設中，製造中；一切如計畫順利進行中

  > The camera company has a new camera **in the works** but nobody knows about it.
  >
  > 相機公司正在製造一種新相機但沒人知道這事。

一般商業片語 (Business Idioms)

- **jack up the price of (something)**：to make a price higher 抬高價格

  The steel company will **jack up the price of** steel at the beginning of the year.
  鋼鐵公司將會在年初抬高鋼鐵價錢。

- **keep books**：to keep records of money that is gained or spent 記帳

  The new sales manager does not know how to **keep books** and he makes many mistakes.
  新經理不知道如何記帳且犯了很多錯誤。

- **keep track of (something)**：to keep account or record of something, to stay informed about something 與…保持聯繫；記住，留意

  We are trying to **keep track of** the number of visitors to our store.
  我們試著記錄下到我們商店裡的訪客數目。

- **a kickback**：an amount of money that is paid illegally for a favorable treatment 回扣

  The construction company was giving **kickbacks** to the local politicians.
  建設公司給當地政治人物回扣。

- **knock down the price of (something)/ knock the price of (something) down**：to lower the price of something 殺價

  I bargained hard so that I could **knock down the price of** the DVD players.
  我努力討價還價為的是能將影音光碟機的價錢砍下來。

一般商業片語 (Business Idioms)

- **land an account**：to acquire an account 得到客戶

  > The salesman **landed a** large **account** on his first day of work.
  > 這個推銷員在第一天上班就得到一個大客戶。

- **lay (something) on the table**：to present a matter for discussion 攤牌

  > I went to the meeting and **laid** my concerns about the new product **on the table**.
  > 我去開會並挑明我對新產品的憂慮。

- **lead time**：the amount of time between the placing an order and the receipt of the goods that one has ordered 時程

  > The **lead time** to get a book published is very long.
  > 要發行一本書的時程相當長。

- **line of products**：a group or category of products that are similar to each other 系列產品

  > Our company will introduce a new **line of products** in the autumn.
  > 我們公司將在秋天引進新的系列產品。

- **liquid assets**：property or belongings that can easily be converted into cash 容易變現的資產，流動資產

  > The company sold some **liquid assets** in order to raise cash.
  > 公司出售一些流動資產來募集現金。

一般商業片語 (Business Idioms)

make a cold call：to visit or telephone a potential but unknown customer from a list of people 隨機打電話給非特定對象查詢意願

> When he first started to work at his company the salesman was asked to **make cold calls** from the telephone book.
>
> 當這個推銷員剛開始在他的公司上班時，他被要求從電話簿中打電話找客戶。

make a go of (something)：to produce good results, to succeed at something 成功

> Although the man works very hard in his small business, he cannot **make a go of** it and may soon go out of business.
>
> 儘管這人在自己的小商店上相當努力，但他似乎無法成功且將很快就關門大吉。

make a motion：to make a suggestion or proposal at a meeting 提案；建議

> The manager **made a motion** to finish the meeting early and continue the next morning.
>
> 經理提議早點結束會議並在明天再繼續。

make an offer：to make a financial proposal for a product or service 提議，提供；出價

> We plan to **make an offer** to buy the house on Saturday.
>
> 我們計畫在週六出價買房子。

一般商業片語 (Business Idioms)

○ **make money hand to fist**：to make a lot of money 賺大錢

> The small ice cream shop has been **making money hand to fist** since it opened.
> 這家小冰淇淋店從開業就一直賺大錢。

○ **mean business**：to be serious 嚴肅正經；玩真的

> Our boss **means business** when he tells everyone to work harder.
> 當我們老闆告訴所有人更努力工作時他是說真的。

○ **move to do (something)**：to propose to do something (usually at a meeting) 提議去做…

> I will **move to** have another meeting next week so that we can discuss the problem.
> 我提議我們下星期再開一個會來討論這個問題。

○ **a number cruncher**：an account, someone who works with numbers 會計，懂得數字遊戲的人

> Our company president is **a good number cruncher** and he understands the finance of our company.
> 我們公司總經理是個懂得數字的人，他對公司財務瞭如指掌。

○ **on hand**：to be in one's possession, to be ready 現成的，手頭上的

> We did not have enough supplies **on hand** so we were unable to finish the job.
> 我們手頭上沒有足夠的文具所以無法完成工作。

一般商業片語 (Business Idioms)

on the block：to be for sale, to go on sale 出售

> After we bought the company we put some of the equipment **on the block**.
> 在收購這間公司後我們出售一些設備。

out-of-pocket expenses：the direct expenses that one must personally pay for 自己掏腰包

> My **out-of-pocket expenses** were very high during the business trip.
> 我這趟出差自己掏腰包的花費很高。

out of stock：not available for immediate sale 沒有庫存

> The toys are **out of stock** and we must wait several weeks before we can get them.
> 玩具沒有庫存而我們必須等幾個禮拜才能得到它們。

outsource (something)：to use outside sources for something rather than those within a company or its facilities 外包

> The manufacturing company **outsourced** much of its work.
> 這家製造商把大部分工作外包。

pay off：to succeed, to yield good results 成功，產生好結果

> I hope that our plans for the new business will **pay off**.
> 我希望我們新事業的計畫會成功。

一般商業片語 (Business Idioms)

◉ **pay off a debt**：to finish paying back the money that one has borrowed from a bank or business or person 還清債務

> The furniture manufacturer was unable to **pay off their loan** so they went out of business.
>
> 家具製造商因無法還清債務而倒閉。

◉ **piece of action**：a share in the activity or the profits of something 分一杯羹；好處

> The inventor wanted a **piece of action** from the new equipment that he had invented.
>
> 發明家想要在他所發明的新設備中分一杯羹。

◉ **plug a product**：to promote a product 促銷

> The soccer star makes a lot of money when he agrees a **plug a product**.
>
> 足球明星因為答應促銷某件商品而賺大錢。

◉ **preferred customer**：a customer who does much business with you and who give special discounts to 優先客戶，享受特別待遇的客戶

> The man is a **preferred customer** and we always give him a good price.
>
> 這人是個好客戶而且我們總是給他好價錢。

◉ **put one's nose to the grindstone**：to work diligently or hard 努力辛勤地工作

> I **put my nose to the grindstone** and finished the job before the weekend.
>
> 我辛苦工作並在週末前完成工作。

P

一般商業片語 (Business Idioms)

saddle with debt：to be burdened with debit 為債務所困

> Our company is **saddled with debt** and must do something about it quickly.
> 我們公司為債務所困而且必須馬上採取行動。

sell like a hotcake：to sell very quickly 熱賣

> The children's toys were **selling like hotcakes** at the end of the year.
> 兒童玩具在年底時熱賣。

sell out：to sell all of a product 產品銷售一空

> Every year our company is able to **sell out** most of our summer goods.
> 每年我們公司都能將大部分的夏季產品銷售一空。

sell (something) at a loss：to sell something and lose money 賠本出售

> We were forced to **sell** the computers **at a loss**.
> 我們被迫賠本賣掉電腦。

set up a meeting：to make arrangement for a meeting 安排會議

> I am trying to **set up a meeting** with the manager of our department.
> 我正在嘗試安排和我們部門經理開一次會。

slice of the action：a share in activity or the profits of something 好處

> The government wanted a **slice of the action** from the new business.
> 政府想在新事業中討好處。

S

一般商業片語 (Business Idioms)

strike while the iron is hot：to take advantage of an opportunity 打鐵趁熱

> I plan to **strike while the iron is hot** and apply for the job quickly.
>
> 我打算打鐵趁熱馬上申請這份工作。

a sweet deal：a deal made between friends or businesses so that both may receive a benefit 雙方都有好處的作法

> We made **a sweet deal** with our landlord to have our rent reduced.
>
> 我們和房東做出降低我們的房租的皆大歡喜的協議。

table a discussion：to postpone a discussion until a later time 暫緩討論

> We **tabled the discussion** about the salary issue until the next meeting.
>
> 我們將薪資議題暫緩到下次會議。

take a nosedive：to collapse, the decrease in vale 崩潰，價值巨幅下滑

> The stock market **took a nosedive** when the earnings of the oil company decreased.
>
> 股票市場因石油公司營收下降而大幅下跌。

take a pay cut：to accept a decrease in one's salary 減薪

> The telephone workers were forced to **take a pay cut** after the strike.
>
> 電話工人在罷工後被迫減薪。

一般商業片語 (Business Idioms)

- **take minutes**：to write down the details of a meeting 做會議紀錄

  I usually **take minutes** at the monthly club meetings.

  我通常在俱樂部每月例會中當紀錄。

- **take on (an employee)/ take (an employee) on**：to give a job to someone, to hire someone 僱用

  The company **took on** many new workers during the busy holiday season.

  公司在繁忙的假期僱用了許多新員工。

- **take a company public**：to sell shares of a company to the general public 股票公開上市

  We decided to **take our company public** in order to raise money to expand our factory.

  我們決定公司股票公開上市以籌募擴充工廠的資金。

- **take over (something)/take (something) over**：to take control or possession of something, to take charge or responsibility of something 接管，接掌

  The government decided to **take over** the bank after it declared bankruptcy.

  政府決定在銀行宣告破產後接管。

- **take (something) at face value**：to take something that is said exactly as it is said 無異議接受他人所說的一切

  I **took** my friend's comment **at face value**.

  我對朋友所說的完全接受。

一般商業片語 (Business Idioms)

take stock：to count the items of merchandise or supplies in stock at a business, to take inventory 清查庫存

> The department store closes for three days every March in order to **take stock**.
> 百貨公司每到三月都會歇業三天來清查庫存。

tall order：a long list of demands 很多要求

> The new manager had a **tall order** ready for his staff the first day he came to work.
> 新經理第一天來上班時就對屬下要求很多。

throw cold water on (something)：to discourage or forbid something 澆冷水

> The manager **threw cold water on** our plan to close the factory for one week in August.
> 經理對我們在八月時關閉工廠一個星期的計畫澆冷水。

throw money at (something)：to try to solve a problem by spending money on it 花大錢解決問題

> The president of our company is willing to **throw much money at** the factory problem.
> 總經理願意在解決工廠問題上花大錢。

tight spot：a difficult situation 困難的處境

> The computer company has been in a **tight spot** since the shortage of computer chips appeared.
> 電腦公司自從晶片短缺起就一直處在困難的狀況中。

T

一般商業片語 (Business Idioms)

turn a profit：to make a profit 賺錢

> The supermarket has been **turning a profit** since it opened.
>
> 超級市場從開張到現在都一直賺錢。

turn over：to do business to a certain amount of money of product 交易，周轉，做…金額的生意

> We **turn over** much of our stock every month.
>
> 我們每個月都交易很多公司的股票。
>
> The company **turns over** much money every week.
>
> 公司每星期都周轉很多錢。

turnover (of a product)：the rate at which a product is sold or replaced 營業收入，交易總額

> The **turnover** of cold drinks is very high in the store.
>
> 店裡冷飲的銷售量很高。

turnover (of worker)：the rate at which employees join and leave a company 流動率

> The **turnover of workers** in the new company is very high.
>
> 新公司員工的流動率很高。

work out：to have a specific result 發揮功用，有效

> I do not think the new plan is going to **work out**.
>
> 我不覺得新計畫會有用。

一般商業片語 (Business Idioms)

work out (a problem)：to solve a problem, to provide the details of something 金額被算出，問題被解決

> I spent the weekend trying to **work out** the budget estimate for next year.
>
> 我把週末花在解決明年預算問題上。

work overtime：to work more than one's regular hours 加班

> I **worked overtime** every Friday last month.
>
> 我上個月每個星期五都加班。

write off (a debt/loan)：to remove a debt/loan from a business record, to cancel a debt 打消債務或借貸

> It was impossible for the bank to collect the money so they were forced to **write off the loan**.
>
> 銀行無法收回金錢所以他們被迫在帳冊上打消借貸。

W

測驗題 (Idiom Quizzes)

Choose an idiom to replace the expression in the blankets:

1. The first company was forced to sell most of its merchandise (although it lost money).

   A by a long shot   B at a loss   C in black and white   D in the long run

2. The price of oil (reaches its lowest point) in July and began to rise soon after.

   A cut corners   B closed out   C broke even   D bottomed out

3. The computer company had much trouble trying to get their new business to (make a successful start).

   A be in the red   B get off the ground   C mean business   D strike while the iron is hot

4. The price of computer chips (collapsed) after personal computer sales began to decrease.

   A took a nosedive   B turned over   C bottomed out   D carried the day

5. The automobile dealer had no trucks (available to sell) so we had to wait for two months to buy one.

   A in the works   B on credit   C in stock   D written off

6. The large drug company (took control of) the small drugstore chain.

   A took over   B took stock of   C turned over   D sold out

7. There is a chance to make much money during the summer so we will (take advantage of the opportunity) and work hard.

   A throw money at it   B strike while the iron is hot   C sell like hotcakes
   D mean business

8. Our plans for marketing the new computer are still (in preparation).

   A coming on strong   B in short supply   C going public   D in the works

9. The bank (cancelled) the loans to the bankrupt company.

   A wrote off   B worked out   C took over   D paid off

10. The construction company (hired) hundreds of new workers last month.

   A took over   B turned over   C took on   D made a go of

11. Our company needed to raise money to expand so we decided to (sell its shares on the stock market).

   A take a nosedive   B sell it out   C take it over   D take it public

12. The steel company finally went bankrupt after being (burdened with loses) for many years.

   A jacked up   B on the block   C saddled with debt   D paid off

13. We are (ready to buy) a new car but we have not found anything that we like.

   A in the loop for　　B in the market for　　C in charge of　　D cutting back

14. The salesman tried to sell the house by (being very aggressive) which made us uncomfortable.

   A a hard sell　　B keeping books　　C a kickback　　D a company man

15. We tried to get a (rough estimate) for the cost of new computer printers.

   A budget crunch　　B number cruncher　　C ball park figure　　D sweet deal

16. We decided to sell business in order to (stop losing money).

   A bottom out　　B mean business　　C cut our losses　　D strike while the iron is hot

17. (Someone will be punished) if we do not quickly deal with the poor sales of our product.

   A Someone will fill the bill　　B Someone will get a break　　C Someone will deliver the goods　　D Heads will roll

18. Gas and oil were (in less than the amount needed) during the busy summer season.

   A in short supply　　B in stock　　C in the works　　D filling the bill

19. The (amount of sales) of computers increased dramatically last year.

   A write-off   B turnover   C calculated risk   D double check

20. We closed the store early in order to (count the number of items we had).

   A take stock   B run short   C work overtime   D gain ground

解答 (Answer Keys)

1. B	2. D	3. B	4. A	5. C
6. A	7. B	8. D	9. A	10. C
11. D	12. C	13. B	14. A	15. C
16. C	17. D	18. A	19. B	20. A

Negotiation Idioms
談判協商交涉片語

談判協商交涉片語 (Negotiation Idioms)

at stake：something that can be gained or lost 有利害關係

> There was much **at stake** during the negotiations between the employees and employers.
>
> 在員工和雇主之間的協商中涉及很多利害關係。

back down：to yield in one's position during negotiations, to not follow up on a threat 軟化；讓步

> The government **backed down** on their threat to give less money to the school district.
>
> 政府在威脅不給學區更多的錢上做了讓步。

back out of (something)：to get out of an agreement, to fail to keep a promise 毀約

> The property developer **backed out of** the plan to build a new apartment building.
>
> 土地開發商毀約不去履行蓋一棟新公寓大樓的計畫。

ball is in (someone's) court：it is the decision of another person or group to do something 由某人或某團體來決定

> The **ball is in** the union's **court** after the company made their final offer.
>
> 在公司做出最後提議後，現在是由工會來做決定了。

beat around the bush：to talk about something without giving a direct answer 閃爍其詞

> The manager was **beating around the bush** and never said anything important.
>
> 經理閃爍其詞避重就輕。

談判協商交涉片語 (Negotiation Idioms)

- **bog down**：to slow down and make no progress (a bog is an area of land that is wet and muddy -like a swamp) 動彈不得，沒有進展 (swamp：溼地)

  The negotiation **bogged down** over the issue of part-time workers.

  協商因為兼職人員的議題而沒有進展。

- **bone of contention**：the subject or reason for a fight or dispute 造成爭吵或爭執的原因

  The size of the project was a **bone of contention** between the city and the developer.

  計畫的規模是市政府和開發商起爭執的原因。

- **break down**：to fail, to stop 失敗，終止

  The negotiation **broke down** last night when both sides refused to compromise.

  協商因雙方拒絕妥協而在昨晚終止。

- **break off (something)/break (something) off**：to stop or end suddenly 中斷；破裂

  The government decided to **break off** talks about extending the trade agreement.

  政府決定中斷延長貿易協定的會談。

- **break through**：to be successful after overcoming a difficulty 突破（動詞）

  We were able to **break through** in our efforts to find a solution to the problem.

  我們可以在尋找問題解決之道上做突破。

談判協商交涉片語 (Negotiation Idioms)

breakthrough：a success that comes after overcoming a difficulty 突破（名詞）

There was a **breakthrough** in the talks to end the teachers' strike.
在終止老師罷工的會談中有了突破。

bring (someone) to terms：to make someone agree to something or do something 使某人投降 [臣服，同意]

The government worked hard to **bring** the two sides **to terms**.
政府努力讓雙方達成協議。

bring up (something)/bring (something) up：to begin a discussion about something, to mention something 開始討論某事，提及某事

I tried to **bring up** the subject of sales commissions during the meeting.
我試著在會議中提到佣金一事。

call someone's bluff：to try to make someone prove that they can actually do what they say they can 說某人唬人或玩假的

The government **called** the union's **bluff** when the union threatened to go on strike.
當工會威脅罷工時，政府說他們是唬人的。

call the shots：to be in charge 對…做決定，發令

During the meeting the vice-president was **calling the shots**.
在會議中，副總經理負責發號施令。

談判協商交涉片語 (Negotiation Idioms)

cave in to (someone/something)：to weaken or be forced to give up 屈服

The company was forced to **cave in to** the demands of the workers for money.
公司被迫對員工要求更多錢一事屈服。

close a deal：to end a negotiation successfully 成功達成協議；做成買賣

We had to work hard but we were finally able to **close the deal**.
雖然我們必須很努力但我們終究能做成生意。

close ranks：to unite and fight together 團結一致

During the meeting we **close ranks** and refused to compromise on any issue.
在會議上我們團結一致拒絕對任何議題做妥協。

come down in price：to lower the price of one's product 降價

We decided to **come down in price** and try and sell our products quickly.
我們決定降價並試著盡快賣出我們的產品。

come in low：to offer a low amount of money for a product or service 出低價

The company **came in low** with an offer for our product.
這家公司對我們的產品出低價。

談判協商交涉片語 (Negotiation Idioms)

- **come to terms**：to reach an agreement 同意

  After negotiating all night the government and the company **came to terms** on an agreement for a new water system.

  在整晚協商後，政府和公司同意新的用水系統。

- **come up in a discussion**：to become a subject in a discussion 變成討論的議題

  Nothing related to the issue of quality **came up in the discussion**.

  在討論中品質一直沒有成為議題。

- **common ground**：shared beliefs or interests 共同點，共識

  There was no **common ground** between the two sides and the negotiation did not go well.

  因雙方無共識所以協商進行並不順利。

- **(continue) down to the wire**：to near a deadline, to have little time remaining 剩下時間不多；最後關頭

  The negotiations **continued down to the wire** but they ended successfully.

  協商一直到最後關頭才圓滿達成。

  They went **down to the wire** but the two sides finally agreed to a new contract.

  雙方到最後才同意新合約。

談判協商交涉片語 (Negotiation Idioms)

- **cover ground**：to talk about the important facts and details of something 所涉及的範圍

  > The questions were endless and we were unable to **cover ground** during the meeting.
  >
  > 問題如此多以至於在會議中我們什麼都沒討論到。

- **cut a deal**：to make an agreement, to make a deal or arrangement 達成協議

  > We **cut a deal** and left the meeting in a positive mood.
  >
  > 我們達成協議並以正面的心情離開會議。

- **cut (someone off)/cut off (someone)**：to stop someone from saying something, to interrupt someone 打斷某人的談話發言

  > My friend **cut** me **off** when I was speaking.
  >
  > 我的朋友在我發言時打斷我。

- **drag on**：to be prolonged, to continue for a long time 拖延；持續很久

  > The talks between the company and the lawyers **dragged on** for several weeks.
  >
  > 公司和律師間的會談拖了好幾個禮拜。

- **drag one's heels**：to act slowly or reluctantly 不情願地

  > The government **dragged their heels** in talks with the union about the new contract.
  >
  > 政府和工會在新合約的協商中顯得不情願。

談判協商交涉片語 (Negotiation Idioms)

draw the line：to set a limit about what will be done or discussed 畫出底線；不妥協讓步

> The union was flexible on the salary issue but they **drew the line** at talking about health benefits.
>
> 公會在薪資議題上相當有彈性但在健康福利上則不讓步。

draw up (something)/draw (something) up：to put something (a contract or a plan) in writing 起草…

> The lawyers **drew up** a contract for the new housing development on the government land.
>
> 律師就在公有地興建國宅一事起草一份新合約。

drive a hard bargain：to bargain and try to make an agreement to one's advantage 討價還價不讓自己吃虧

> The sales manager **drives a hard bargain** and it is difficult to negotiate with him.
>
> 業務經理很強硬，所以和他協商很困難。

drive at (something)：to mean something, to want to say something 有…意思，想要說…

> I could not understand what the other negotiators in the meeting were **driving at**.
>
> 我無法了解其他協商者想要的是什麼。

談判協商交涉片語 (Negotiation Idioms)

- **face down (someone)/face (someone) down**：to confront someone boldly 直接了當地面對他人

  The government decided to **face down** the striking transportation workers.
  政府決定對罷工的運輸工人攤牌。

- **fall through**：to fail, to be ruined, to not happen 失敗，未能實現

  The deal of new machinery **fell through** and we will have to look for another supplier.
  新機器的交易失敗而我們必須另找供應商。

- **fifty-fifty**：equally, evenly 均分

  We shared the profits with the other company **fifty-fifty**.
  我們和另一家公司平分利潤。

- **follow through on [with] (something)**：to finish an action, to keep a promise 後續

  Our boss said that wages would improve soon but he never **followed through with** his promise.
  老闆說薪水會很快改進但他從沒任何後續動作。

- **force someone's hand**：to make someone do something that they do not want to do at that time 強迫

  We decided to **force our opponent's hand** because we wanted to finish the negotiation quickly.
  我們決定去強迫對手，因我們想要趕快結束協商。

談判協商交涉片語 (Negotiation Idioms)

- **get behind a person [an idea]**：to support a person or idea 支持某人 [某事]

  > Although we did not agree with the manager, we **got behind** his proposal at the meeting.
  >
  > 雖然我們不同意經理，但我們在會議中仍然支持他的提案。

- **get down to brass tacks**：to begin to work or business that must be done 做真正重要的事

  > Let's **get down to brass tacks** and begin talking about the new contract.
  >
  > 讓我們開始討論重要的事：新合約。

- **get down to business**：to start working or doing the business at hand 言歸正傳開始做事

  > We must **get down to business** and finish our work quickly.
  >
  > 我們該言歸正傳把我們的工作趕緊完成。

- **get the ball rolling**：to start an activity or action 開始行動

  > We should **get the ball rolling** and begin the meeting at once.
  >
  > 我們應該立即開始會議。

- **get the message**：to understand clearly what someone means 了解對方的意思

  > I do not think that the opposite side **got the message** about where the negotiation are heading.
  >
  > 我不覺得對方了解交涉磋商的方向為何。

談判協商交涉片語 (Negotiation Idioms)

get to first base：to make a good start, to succeed 好的開始

> We have been able to **get to first base** regarding the terms of the new contract.
>
> 在新合約的條件上我們能夠有好的開始。

get to the bottom of (something)：to discover or understand the real cause of something 追根究柢

> It will be difficult to **get to the bottom of** the financial problems in the company.
>
> 要在公司的財務問題上追根究柢是件困難的事。

get to the heart of (something)：to find the most important facts or central meaning of something 抓到重心，癥結

> We spent the morning trying to **get to the heart of** the problem with the computer supplier.
>
> 我們花了一上午試著找到和電腦供應商之間問題的癥結。

give a little：to compromise during a negotiation 稍做讓步

> We know that we must **give a little** if we want to complete the negotiation.
>
> 我們知道如果我們要完成協商的話必須稍做讓步。

give and take [give-and-take]：to share, to give up of what you want in order to make an agreement 妥協，遷就

> After much **give and take** we reached an agreement regarding the property transfer.
>
> 在一番妥協後我們針對財產轉移做出協議。

- **give ground**：to move back or retreat from one's position 退讓，退卻，失利

  > We bargained hard but the other sales representative refused to **give ground**.
  > 我們努力討價還價但對方業務代表拒絕讓步。

- **give in (to someone)**：to do what another person wants rather than to fight and argue with him or her 投降，讓步

  > After eight weeks of negotiation we **gave in** and agreed to sell the machinery at a discount.
  > 經過八週的協商後我們讓步並以折扣價賣出機具。

- **go back to (someone)**：to not be faithful or loyal to one's word or an agreement 食言

  > The company directors **went back on** their word to give the employees a salary increase.
  > 公司董事們在給員工加薪一事上食言。

- **go back to the drawing board**：to go back and start something from the beginning 重新開始

  > The negotiation failed so we had to **go back to the drawing board** and start over.
  > 協商失敗所以我們必須重新開始。

- **go down to the wire**：to near the deadline, the have little time remaining 最後關頭；餘時不多

  > The negotiations **went down to the wire** last night.
  > 昨晚協商到了最後關頭。

談判協商交涉片語 (Negotiation Idioms)

- **go for broke**：to risk everything on one big effort, to try as hard as possible 孤注一擲；盡最大努力

  > After **going for broke** at the meeting, we were able to reach an agreement.
  > 在會議中孤注一擲後我們終能達成協議。

- **go over well with**：to be liked or successful 收效，得好評

  > My idea about employee evaluations **went over well with** the manager.
  > 我在員工評鑑上的點子得到經理的好評。

- **hammer out (an agreement or a deal)**：to negotiate a deal or agreement by discussion and debate 苦心想出計畫，絞盡腦汁解決問題

  > The negotiations lasted all night but finally we were able to **hammer out an agreement**.
  > 協商持續整晚但我們終於絞盡腦汁達成協議。

- **hang in the balance**：to have two equally possible results, to be uncertain 結果未定，生死未卜

  > The outcome of the election was **hanging in the balance** after the top candidates had an equal number of votes.
  > 選舉結果因領先的候選人票數相當而不確定。

- **hard-nosed**：to be very strict, to be stubborn, to be uncompromising 嚴格；固執；不讓步

  > The negotiators were **hard-nosed** during talks for a new contract.
  > 在新合約的會談中協商者都不讓步。

H

談判協商交涉片語 (Negotiation Idioms)

have a card up one's sleeve：to hide something of value 袖裡乾坤

> I thought that the negotiations would not succeed but my boss **had a card up his sleeve** that we did not know about.
>
> 我以為協商不會成功但我的老闆有我們所不知的法寶。

have a poker face：to not show any reaction or emotion 板著臉，嚴肅

> Our boss **had a poker face** when he told us that our office would soon close.
>
> 我們老闆嚴肅地告訴我們辦公室將很快地就會關門。

hold all the aces [cards, trumps]：to have all the advantages 占盡優勢

> The management group was **holding all the aces** during the meeting with the union.
>
> 公司經營團隊在和工會的磋商中占盡優勢。

hold out for (something)：to keep resisting or refuse to give up until you get the desired results 有所保留

> The union is **holding out for** a better deal and they do not plan to end their strike.
>
> 工會為了要有更好的待遇而有所保留而且他們也不計畫停止罷工。

hold out on (someone)：to refuse to give information or something to someone who has a right to it 扣押該交出的東西

> The new manager has been **holding out on** the company and he will not tell anyone his plan.
>
> 新經理對公司有所隱瞞，他將不會把計畫告訴任何人。

談判協商交涉片語 (Negotiation Idioms)

⊙ **horse-trade**：to make a business agreement or deal after careful bargaining and compromise 討價還價後的結果

> After several hours of **horse-trading** we reached an agreement to buy the new computers.
>
> 在幾個小時的討價還價後我們做出購買新電腦的協議。

⊙ **in the bag**：to be certain 確實無疑，穩操勝算

> The contract for the new insurance policy is **in the bag**.
>
> 新保單的合約已經確定了。

⊙ **iron (something) out/iron out (something)**：to solve a problem 消除困難；使…圓滑

> We spent several hours **ironing out** the final details of the contract.
>
> 我們花了幾個小時來使合約的最後細節更平順。

⊙ **knock down the price of (something)**：to decrease a price 砍價，削價

> The department store has **knocked down the price of** many of their products.
>
> 百貨公司將削減它們許多商品的價錢。

⊙ **lay one's cards on the table**：to be open and honest about one's intentions 攤牌，開誠布公

> Our boss **laid his cards on the table** during the meeting.
>
> 我們老闆在會議上開誠布公。

談判協商交涉片語 (Negotiation Idioms)

make an offer：to make a financial or other proposal for a product or service 提供商品或服務，出價

> I will **make an offer** and try to buy the house that I like.
> 我會對我喜歡的房子出價。

make headway：to make progress 有進展，有進步

> We are bargaining hard and **making headway** with the new agreement.
> 我們在新協定上努力討價還價並有了進展。

meet (someone) halfway：to compromise with someone 對某人妥協 [讓步]

> The price for the truck was too high but we **met** the salesman **halfway** and made an agreement to buy it.
> 卡車的價錢太貴了，但我們和業務員做出協議並同意買它。

nail (something) down/nail down (something)：to make certain or sure 確定

> We **nailed down** an agreement to build the staff room as soon as possible.
> 我們確定要盡快給工作人員蓋一間房間。

off the record：to be not published or revealed, to be a secret 私底下，非公開

> I told my boss **off the record** that I would probably not return after the summer holiday.
> 我私底下告訴老闆我在暑假後很可能不回來工作了。

談判協商交涉片語 (Negotiation Idioms)

- **paint oneself into a corner**：to get into a bad situation that is difficult or impossible to escape 作繭自縛

  > The negotiations became easier when the other side **painted themselves into a corner**.
  >
  > 協商在對方作繭自縛後變得容易許多。

- **play hardball (with someone)**：to act strong and aggressive with someone 強勢

  > The union **played hardball** during the contract talks.
  >
  > 公會在合約協商中採取強硬姿態。

- **play into someone's hand**：to do something that another person can use against you 授人口實，給人藉口

  > Our manager **played into the hands** of the other side when he became angry during the meeting.
  >
  > 我們經理在會議中發怒而給了對方藉口。

- **play one's cards close to one's chest**：to be secretive and cautious about something 小心翼翼，戒慎

  > My colleague was **playing his cards close to his chest** when he began to talk to our competitor.
  >
  > 我的同事在和競爭對手談話時變得小心翼翼。

P

談判協商交涉片語 (Negotiation Idioms)

- **pull (something) off/pull off (something)**：to succeed in doing something difficult or impossible 僥倖成功；得逞

  > The contract seemed impossible to win but we **pulled** it **off** through our skillful maneuver.
  >
  > 我們似乎不可能贏得合約，但在巧妙的運作下我們得逞了。

- **raise the ante**：to increase what is at stake or under discussion in a dispute or conflict 增加賭注

  > The small country **raised the ante** in the trade dispute with other countries.
  >
  > 這個小國家在和他國之間的貿易糾紛中提高賭注。

- **a raw deal**：treatment that is not fair 不公平待遇

  > The sales manager received **a raw deal** when he was forced to give up his former position.
  >
  > 業務經理在被迫放棄先前工作時受到不公平待遇。

- **reach a stalemate**：to arrive at a position where no progress is being made 僵持不下，束手無策

  > The talks to buy new computers have **reached a stalemate** and it will be difficult to start it again.
  >
  > 購買新電腦的談判僵持不下，要重新開始將會很困難。

R

談判協商交涉片語 (Negotiation Idioms)

- **read between the lines**：to understand the meaning of something by guessing what is not said 推敲，在字裡行間找線索

  > The salesman did not say that no products were available but we could **read between the lines** and we knew there were none available.
  >
  > 雖然業務員並未說缺貨，但我們推論現在沒有現貨。

- **rock-bottom offer**：the lowest price that one can offer to buy something 最低價

  > The buyer made a **rock-bottom offer** to buy our products.
  >
  > 買家出最低價來購買我們的產品。

- **a setback**：a change from better to worse, a delay, a reversal 挫折

  > The bad weather was **a setback** in our efforts to get the material delivered on time.
  >
  > 壞天氣使得我們準時送交物品的計畫受挫。

- **smooth (something) over/smooth over (something)**：to make something seem better or less severe 調停，緩頰

  > We tried to **smooth over** the problem between the two managers.
  >
  > 我們試著調停兩位經理之間的問題。

- **stack the deck against (someone)**：to trick someone, to arrange things unfairly 對某人極為不利

  > The manager **stacked the deck against** his opponent when he went into the meeting.
  >
  > 經理在進入會議時決定要對他的對手不利。

S

談判協商交涉片語 (Negotiation Idioms)

- **stand one's ground**：to maintain and defend one's position 堅持立場

  The other negotiation team was very aggressive but we **stood our ground** and bargained hard.

  協商中對方團隊相當積極但我們終能堅守立場並討價還價。

- **stick one's gun**：to defend an action or opinion despite an unfavorable reaction 堅持立場，堅守主張

  We **stuck to our guns** during the meeting and asked for more time to consider the proposal.

  我們在會議中堅持立場並要求有更多時間來考慮此提案。

- **take sides**：to join one group against another in a debate or quarrel 在爭議中選邊站

  I did not **take sides** in the discussion about buying a new computer.

  我在購買新電腦一事中並沒有傾向哪一邊。

- **talk (someone) into (something)**：to get someone to agree to something, to persuade someone to do something 說服某人去做某事

  We were unable to **talk** the other members of our team **into** delaying the meeting until next week.

  我們未能說服團隊中其他成員將會議延遲到下星期。

T

談判協商交涉片語 (Negotiation Idioms)

- **talk (someone) out of (something)**：to persuade someone not to do something 說服某人不去做某事

  I tried to **talk** our sales manager **out of** offering a price for the product that was too low.

  我說服我們業務經理不要對產品出過低的價格。

- **talk (something) over/talk over (something)**：to discuss something 商量

  We asked for some time during the meeting to **talk over** the new proposal.

  我們在會議中要求一些時間來商量新的提案。

- **throw (someone) a curve (ball)**：to mislead or deceive someone 誤導欺騙；出奇不意

  The purchasing manager **threw** us **a curve** when he said he would not need any of our products until next year.

  採購經理出奇不意地告訴我們他們到明年之前都不需要我們任何的產品。

- **to the letter**：exactly, nothing done wrong or left undone; perfectly 精準完美地，一點差錯都沒有

  The union representative followed the contract agreement **to the letter**.

  工會代表一板一眼地遵循合約協議。

T

談判協商交涉片語 (Negotiation Idioms)

- **trump card**：something that is kept back to be used to win success when nothing else works 王牌

  > Although we appeared weak during the negotiations we had some new information to use as our **trump card**.
  >
  > 雖然在協商中我們看起來有些弱，但我們也有些可用的新資訊來充當我們的王牌。

- **undercut (someone)**：to sell your product for less than a competitor 以比對手低的價位賣出產品

  > The new discount store is trying hard to **undercut** other stores in this area.
  >
  > 新的折扣商店試著用本區中最低的價位賣出貨品。

- **water (something) down/water down (something)**：to change or make something weaker 用水沖淡，淡化

  > The manager tried to **water down** our proposal for the new quality control system.
  >
  > 經理試著淡化我們新品質管制制度的企劃的重要性。

- **wheel and deal**：to negotiate to buy or sell something (often in a way that is very close to being dishonest or illegal) 周旋，工於心計

  > The salesman likes to **wheel and deal** with his customers.
  >
  > 這名業務員喜歡和客戶玩心機。

W

談判協商交涉片語 (Negotiation Idioms)

- **wind up (something)/wind (something) up**：to end, to finish, to end 結束，收場

  We would like to **wind up** the meeting early tomorrow.
  明天我們想早點結束會議。

- **wrap up (something)/wrap (something) up**：to finish something (a job, a meeting, etc.) 結束

  We **wrapped up** the meeting and went home for the weekend.
  我們結束會議回家過週末。

W

測驗題 (Idiom Quizzes)

Choose an idiom to replace the expression in the brackets:

1. The negotiation (slowed to a stop) because of the salary issue.

   A broke through   B bogged down   C closed ranks   D get down to business

2. The junior salesman was (in charge) during the meeting.

   A driving a hard bargain   B getting the message   C dragging the heels
   D calling the shot

3. We were told (confidently) that the company was having financial problems.

   A off the record   B standing our ground   C to the letter   D under the wire

4. After thirty hours of bargaining we were able to (make an agreement).

   A get down to business   B cave in   C cut a deal   D paint ourselves into a corner

5. We worked very hard to (find a solution to) the problem with the computer supplier.

   A drag on   B turn thumbs down on   C iron out   D break off

6. We read everything (exactly) before we signed the contract.

   A fifty-fifty   B off the record   C under the wire   D to the letter

7. After seven weeks of negotiations an agreement was (certain).

   A watered down   B in the bag   C read between the lines   D called off

8. The negotiating team worked very hard to (discuss and finalize) a contract with the new company.

   A hammer out   B go back to   C smooth over   D water down

9. After talks failed we were forced to (go back to the beginning).

   A stand out ground   B make headway   C go back to drawing board
   D hang in the balance)

10. In the end we (rejected) the proposal that the company made.

   A turned thumb down on   B watered down   C nailed down   D wrapped up

11. We decided to abandon the project when the negotiations (failed).

   A dragged on   B faced down   C played into our hands   D fell through

12. We bargained hard at the meeting but we were unable to (succeed) with our opponents.

   A give ground   B get to first base   C drive a hard bargain   D take sides

測驗題 (Idiom Quizzes)

13. We (finished) our work and went home early.

    A smoothed over   B talked over   C wrapped up   D followed up

14. During the meeting I (got into a bad situation) which was very difficult to deal with.

    A painted myself into a corner   B got down to brass tacks   C came to terms
    D started the ball rolling

15. The new contract was a major (reason for a dispute) between the workers and the company.

    A setback   B trump card   C rock-bottom offer   D bone of contention

16. The negotiators continued talking (until the deadline).

    A hard-nosed   B down to the wire   C at stake   D fifty-fifty

17. Everyone at the meeting had forgotten about the salary dispute until it was (mentioned) by our boss.

    A brought up   B called off   C faced down   D watered down

18. We spent several days last week trying to (put in writing) the new contract.

    A drag on   B wind up   C draw up   D break through

測驗題 (Idiom Quizzes)

19. There was much (to be gained or lost) when we began the discussion of the new contract.

   A under the wire   B smoothed over   C common ground   D at stake

20. Our opponents tried to (mislead us) during the meeting.

   A come to terms   B throw us a curve   C meet us halfway   D force our hand

21. The salesman complained that he had received (unfair treatment) from his boss.

   A a setback   B a horse trade   C a raw deal   D a card up in his sleeve

22. Our boss is very careful not to (choose one side) in an argument among staff.

   A close ranks   B beat around the bush   C lay his cards on the table   D take sides

23. The members of the group refused to (change their position) during the negotiation.

   A give ground   B break through   C go for broke   D reach a stalemate

24. The members of the committee (supported) our proposal to have a vote.

   A nailed down   B cut off   C got behind   D talked over

25. We (made sure of) the date for the annual meeting.

A smoothed over　　B nailed down　　C watered down　　D drove at

解答 (Answer Keys)

1.	B	2.	D	3.	C	4.	C	5.	D
6.	B	7.	A	8.	C	9.	A	10.	A
11.	B	12.	C	13.	A	14.	B	15.	B
16.	A	17.	C	18.	D	19.	B	20.	B
21.	D	22.	A	23.	C	24.	B	25.	B

Money Idioms
金錢相關片語

金錢相關片語 (Money Idioms)

above par：more than average, above normal, more than the face value of a bond or stock or currency 物超所值

> The currency was selling **above par** at the small exchange shop.
>
> 這種貨幣在這家小的兌換店裡以好價位賣出。

almighty dollar：money when it is viewed as more important than anything else 萬能的金錢

> The man spent most of his life chasing the **almighty dollar**.
>
> 這個人大半輩子都在追求萬能的金錢。

ante up：to pay money, to produce a necessary amount of money 付出

> I had to **ante up** a lot of money to get my car fixed.
>
> 為了修車我必須付出很多錢。

as phony as a three-dollar bill：phony, not genuine 假的

> The man who was asking for donation for the charity was **as phony as a three-dollar bill**.
>
> 這個被要求捐款的人是個空心大老倌。

as poor as a church mouse：very poor 一貧如洗

> The young mother is **as poor as a church mouse** and she has little money to feed her family.
>
> 這女人一貧如洗，她那點錢連養家都不夠。

金錢相關片語 (Money Idioms)

as sound as a dollar：very secure and dependable 安全可靠

The company president believes that his business is **as sound as a dollar**.
公司總經理相信他的生意是相當健全的。

at a premium：at a higher price than usual because of something special 高價

The tickets for the final basketball game were selling **at a premium**.
籃球決賽的門票以高價售出。

at all costs：at any expense of time or effort or money 不計代價

We plan to send our child to a good school **at all costs**.
我們決定不計任何代價把小孩送到好學校。

back on one's feet：to return to good financial health 在經濟上重新站起來

My sister is **back on her feet** after losing her job last year.
我姊姊在去年失掉工作後重新站起來。

balance the books [accounts]：to make sure that all money is accounted for by using generally accepted accounting methods 使帳冊或戶頭收支平衡

The small business owner works very hard to **balance the books** of her company.
這個小生意人努力使她的帳冊收支平衡。

金錢相關片語 (Money Idioms)

⊙ **below par**：lower than average, below normal, less than the face value of a bond or stock or currency 低於平均的價值

> The government bonds were sold at a price that was **below par**.
>
> 政府以低於一般價錢的價格賣出債券。

⊙ **bet on the wrong horse**：to base one's plans on a wrong guess about the results of something 押錯寶

> We are **betting on the wrong horse** if we continue to support the other candidate for mayor.
>
> 如果我們繼續支持另一位市長候選人的話，我們就押錯寶了。

⊙ **bet one's bottom dollar**：to bet all that one has on something because you are sure that you will win 因有把握而把所有錢都賭上

> I would **bet my bottom dollar** that the accounting manager will be late again today.
>
> 我願把我所有的錢都賭在會計經理今天會再一次遲到這件事上。

⊙ **beyond one's means**：more than one can afford 入不敷出

> The young man was living **beyond his means** before he got his first job.
>
> 這年輕人在得到第一個工作前的生活是入不敷出。

⊙ **born with a sliver spoon in one's mouth**：coming from a well-to-do or a pretigious family 出生於富貴之家

> The new student in our class was **born with a silver spoon in his mouth** and he has had an easy life.
>
> 我們班上的新學生出生於富貴之家，而且他的日子過得非常舒適。

金錢相關片語 (Money Idioms)

bread and butter：one's income, the source of someone's food 賴以維生的收入

> The man's business is his **bread and butter** and he works very hard to make it successful.
>
> 這個人的生意是他賴以維生的收入所以他非常努力地讓它成功。

break the bank：to win all the money at a casino gambling table; to use all one's money 在賭場中大贏；贏光所有的錢

> The man **broke the bank** at the casino and walked away with much money.
>
> 這個人在賭場中大贏帶走許多錢。

bring home the bacon：to earn the family living, to earn a salary 養家糊口，賺薪水

> I have been working hard all month **bringing home the bacon** for my family.
>
> 我整個月辛苦工作為了賺得養家的薪水。

burn a hole in one's pocket：to stimulate someone to spend money quickly 守不住財

> The money was **burning a hole in the man's pocket** when he decided to go to the casino.
>
> 當這個人去賭場時他守不住財。

buy off (someone)/buy (someone) off：to give money to someone to stop them from doing their duty 收買

> The man tried to **buy off** the police but the police refused to agree to the plan.
>
> 這個人試著收買警察但警察拒絕他的計畫。

金錢相關片語 (Money Idioms)

buy (something) for a song：to buy something cheaply 廉價買進

I was able to **buy** my first house **for a song**.
我能廉價買進我的第一棟房子。

by check：by using a check 使用支票

I paid for the hotel room **by check**.
我用支票支付旅館費用。

can take (something) to the bank：a statement is true, something is guaranteed to be successful 打包票

I believe that we **can take** the new business plan **to the bank**.
我相信這個新的生意計畫沒有問題。

cash-and-carry：selling something for cash only and with no delivery 現金交易自行提貨

We were able to get a good price on a sofa in a **cash-and-carry** deal at the furniture store.
我們在家具店因現金交易且自行提貨而能省下不少錢。

cash in (something)/cash (something) in：to exchange coupons or bonds for their value in money 兌現，結算，了斷某一件事；死亡

The former basketball player **cashed in** on his popularity to open a very successful restaurant.
前任籃球球員利用他的受歡迎的程度開了家成功的餐廳。

The old man finally **cashed in** after being ill for so long.
老人在久病之後終於走了。

金錢相關片語 (Money Idioms)

- **cash in one's chips**：to exchange or sell something to get some money 求現

  I decided to **cash in my chips** and go back to school.
  我決定賣掉所有東西再回到學校。

- **cash on the barrelhead**：money paid in cash when something is bought 現金

  I gave the salesman **cash on the barrelhead** for the used car.
  我用現金向業務員買舊車。

- **be caught short**：to not have enough money when you need it 短缺金錢

  I **was caught short** and had to borrow some money from my father last week.
  我上週缺錢而且必須向我父親借錢。

- **cheapskate**：a person who will not spend much money, a stingy person 小氣鬼

  My friend is a **cheapskate** and will not go to a movie with me.
  我的朋友是個小氣鬼而且不願意和我去看電影。

- **chicken feed**：a small amount of money 小意思，小錢

  The amount of money that I paid for the used car was **chicken feed**.
  我花在舊車的錢是小錢。

C

金錢相關片語 (Money Idioms)

- **chip in (money)**：to contribute money for something, to pay jointly for something 集資，湊錢

  > Everybody in our office **chipped in** some money to buy a wedding present for our secretary.
  >
  > 我們辦公室裡的所有人湊錢為祕書買件結婚禮物。

- **chisel (someone) out of (something)**：to cheat someone to get money or something 欺騙；詐取

  > The criminal tried to **chisel** the small business owner **out of** much money.
  >
  > 這名罪犯試著向小生意人詐騙。

- **clean up**：to make a lot of money, to make a big profit 賺大錢；清光

  > I **cleaned up** at the horse races last year and I still have some money left.
  >
  > 我去年在賽馬中大勝，到現在我還剩下些錢。

- **closefisted (with money)**：to be very stingy with money 手頭守得很緊

  > The man is **closefisted with money** and will not spend it.
  >
  > 這個人手很緊不會亂花錢。

- **cold hard cash**：cash or coins or bills 現金

  > I paid for the stereo in **cold hard cash**.
  >
  > 我用現金買音響。

金錢相關片語 (Money Idioms)

- **control the purse strings**：to be in charge of the money in a business or household 在公司或家中管錢的人

  My sister **controls the purse strings** in her family.

  我姊姊家裡的錢由她管。

- **cook the books [accounts]**：to illegally change information in the accounting books in a company, to write down false numbers in the accounting books in a company 竄改帳目

  The accountant was **cooking the books** for more than one year before he was caught.

  會計在被抓到前已經竄改帳簿一年多了。

- **cost a pretty penny**：to cost a lot of money 花了相當多的錢

  It is going to **cost a pretty penny** to get my car fixed.

  要把我的車修好將會花一筆大錢。

- **cost an arm and a leg**：to cost a lot of money 花了很多錢；價格昂貴

  My new television **cost an arm and a leg**.

  我的電視機很貴。

- **cross someone's palm with silver**：to give money to someone in payment for a service 付錢給人；賄賂某人

  We had to **cross** the apartment manager's **palm with silver** in order to rent the apartment.

  我們必須付錢給公寓經理以便租到公寓。

C

金錢相關片語 (Money Idioms)

cut one's losses：to reduce one's losses of money or something else 減少損失

> The owners decided to sell the soccer team in order to **cut their losses**.
> 足球隊老闆們決定賣掉足球隊以減少損失。

cut someone a check：to write a check (usually used for a company which automatically produces a check with a computer) 開支票

> The company **cut me a check** to pay for my extra work.
> 公司為了我額外的工作而開支票給我。

cut someone off without a penny：to stop giving someone a regular amount of money, to leave someone no money in a will 停止津貼；在遺囑中除名

> The wealthy businessman **cut his son off without a penny** when the young man refused to work hard.
> 這個有錢的生意人在他兒子拒絕努力工作後停止給他錢。

cut-rate：a price that is lower than usual 削價的；打折的

> We went to a **cut-rate** store to buy some new furniture for our apartment.
> 我們到折扣商店去給我們的公寓買些新家具。

deadbeat：a person who never pays the money that he or she owes 賴債者

> Recently, the government is trying to solve the problem of **deadbeat** fathers who do not support their families.
> 最近政府在試著解決不去養家但又賴債的父親們的問題。

金錢相關片語 (Money Idioms)

- **a dime a dozen**：easy to get and therefore of little value 不值錢的

  Used computers are **a dime a dozen** and they have little value.
  舊電腦不值錢而且它們也沒價值。

- **dirt cheap**：extremely cheap 賤如糞土的，非常便宜的

  The land was **dirt cheap** when we bought it.
  當我們買這土地時它很便宜。

- **dollar for dollar**：considering the cost 考慮成本價值

  Dollar for dollar the new hotel is the best bargain in the city for tourists.
  考慮所付出的錢時，這家新旅館是觀光客最好的選擇。

- **down-and-out**：have no money 落魄潦倒的

  My friend was **down-and-out** for many years before he got a job.
  我的朋友在找到工作前已經落魄潦倒許多年了。

- **draw interest**：for money to earn interest while it is on deposit at a bank 把錢放在銀行裡孳息

  We put money into our bank account so that it would **draw interest**.
  我們把錢放在銀行戶頭中生息。

金錢相關片語 (Money Idioms)

Dutch treat：a situation where each person pays his or her own share of the expenses 各付各

> The movie was a **Dutch treat** so that I did not have to pay for my date.
> 電影是各付各的所以我不必替我的伴侶付錢。

easy money：money that you do not need to work hard to get 輕鬆容易賺的錢

> I was able to make some **easy money** from my job during the summer.
> 我在暑期中賺了些輕鬆錢。

a fast buck：money that is earned quickly and easily (and sometimes dishonestly) 快且容易賺的錢（通常是不老實的）

> The company tried to make **a fast buck** on the property but actually they lost a lot of money.
> 公司想在土地上馬上賺錢但實際上他們反倒賠大錢。

feed the kitty：to contribute money to a special collection 為某特定目的聚資

> Everybody had to **feed the kitty** in order to collect money for the party.
> 所有人都要為了公司聚會而出錢。

feel like a million dollars [bucks]：to feel wonder, to feel well and healthy 感覺很棒

> Although I have been sick for a few weeks, I **feel like a million dollars** today.
> 儘管我病了幾個禮拜，我今天感覺很好。

金錢相關片語 (Money Idioms)

flat broke：to have no money at all 完全破產

> I am **flat broke** and do not have enough money to pay my rent.
> 我完全破產沒錢付房租。

float a loan：to get a loan, to arrange for a loan 貸款

> I decided to **float a loan** to get some money to buy a car.
> 我決定貸款買車。

a fool and his money are soon parted：if a person acts unwisely with money he or she will soon lose it 因愚蠢而喪失錢財

> **A fool and his money are soon parted** when the young man got the money from his father he soon spent it.
> 這年輕人從他父親處得到錢到很快就花光；理財不慎的人很快就會和錢說再見。

foot the bill：to pay for something 付錢

> My sister will **foot the bill** for her daughter's education if she decides to go to the university.
> 我姊姊會替她女兒付錢，如果她決定去讀大學。

for a song：at a low price, cheaply 極少代價；便宜的

> We bought the car **for a song** and will use it in our holiday.
> 我們花了很少錢買車並將在假期時使用它。

金錢相關片語 (Money Idioms)

- **(not) for love or money**：not for anything, not for any price (usually used in the negative) 任何代價都不夠

  I would **not** want to have the man's job **for love or money**.

  不論任何代價我都不會要這個人的工作。

- **for my money**：used before you say something to show that it is your opinion 在表達自己意見前的開場白

  For my money, I believe that the new company policy will not be successfully.

  就我意見而言，新公司的政策不會成功。

- **for peanuts**：very little money 為極少代價

  The man had no money and was willing to work **for peanuts**.

  這人沒錢；他願意為很低的代價工作。

- **fork out money (for something)/fork money out (for something)**：to pay for something 付出

  I had to **fork out much money** to get my car fixed.

  我必須為修車而付出很多錢。

- **fork over (some money)/fork (some money) over**：to pay money for something 為某事或某物付錢

  I **forked over** much money for the painting that is hanging on my wall.

  我為牆上掛的畫付出很多錢。

金錢相關片語 (Money Idioms)

- **free and clear**：(to own something) completely and without owing any money 沒有欠錢

  > My neighbor owns his house **free and clear**.
  > 我的鄰居在他所擁有的房子上沒有任何債務。

- **from rags to riches**：from poverty to wealth 從一貧如洗到富可敵國

  > The man went **from rags to riches** with his hard work.
  > 這人因努力工作而由貧至富。

- **get a run for one's money /give someone a run for the money**：to receive a challenge, to receive what one deserves 面對挑戰；為所得到的代價而付出

  > The man **got a run for his money** when he decided to volunteer for the project.
  > 這人因決定自願做這個計畫而讓人覺得他不是只拿錢而不做事。

- **get along on a shoestring**：to be able to live on very little money 勉強過日子

  > The woman was forced to **get along on a shoestring** when she was a student.
  > 這女人在學生時代被迫過苦日子。

- **get one's money worth**：to get everything (or even a little more) that one has paid for 一分錢一分貨；物超所值

  > We **got our money's worth** when we were able to spend the day at the water park.
  > 我們在水上樂園所花的時間是值回票價。

金錢相關片語 (Money Idioms)

- **give someone a blank check**：to let someone act as they want or as they think is necessary 讓自由處理；放手讓人去做某事

  > The city **gave** the department **a blank check** to try and solve the homeless problem.
  >
  > 市政府放手讓負責部門去解決遊民的問題。

- **go broke**：to lose all of one's money, to become bankrupt 破產

  > My friend started a company last year but it quickly **went broke**.
  >
  > 我朋友去年開了一間公司但很快就破產了。

- **go Dutch**：to share in the cost of a meal or some other event 各付各的

  > We decided to **go Dutch** when we went to the restaurant for dinner.
  >
  > 在去餐廳用晚餐時我們決定各付各的。

- **give (someone) a run for their money**：to give someone a challenge, to give someone what they deserve 得到付出代價後的報償；激烈的競爭

  > The young candidate for the city park board **gave** the more experienced candidate **a run for his money** during the election.
  >
  > 競選城市公園管理處委員的年輕候選人讓有經驗的老將在選舉時苦戰一場。

- **go to the expense (of doing something)**：to pay the cost of doing something 花錢去…

  > I don't want to **go to the expense** of buying a new sofa for our apartment.
  >
  > 我不想花錢為我們的公寓裡買套新沙發。

金錢相關片語 (Money Idioms)

- **going rate**：the current rate 市價

  The **going rate** for a used bicycle is not very much.
  二手腳踏車的市價並不貴。

- **gravy train**：a job or some work that pays more than it is worth 肥缺

  The job was a **gravy train** and I made a lot of money when I worked there.
  我在那裡工作時，那個工作是個肥缺，我也賺了許多錢。

- **grease someone's palm/grease the palm of someone**：a pay for a special favor or for extra help, to bribe someone 收買；賄賂

  We had to **grease the palm of** the hotel manager to get a room.
  我們得賄賂旅館經理才能有個房間。

- **a handout**：a gift money (usually from the government) 施捨

  The bus company has received many **handouts** from the government.
  公車公司收了許多政府的補助。

- **hard up**：to not have much money 很窮，缺乏

  The man is **hard up** for money and he often wants to borrow some.
  這人總是缺錢而且他總是要借錢。

- **have an itch [itchy] palm**：to ask for tips or money 貪賄，貪財；要小費

  The hotel clerk **has an itchy palm** and he is always asking for money.
  旅館職員很愛錢而他也總是伸手要錢。

金錢相關片語 (Money Idioms)

- **have money to burn**：to have very much money, to have more money than is needed 有很多錢

  My aunt **has money to burn** and she is always traveling somewhere.

  我嬸嬸很有錢，她總是四處旅行。

- **have one's hand in the till**：to be stealing money from a company or an organization 偷錢，手腳不乾淨

  The clerk **had her hand in the till** so we decided to fire her.

  這個職員偷錢所以我們決定開除她。

- **have sticky fingers**：to be a thief 做賊

  The new employee **has sticky fingers** and many things in the store have disappeared.

  這個新員工是個賊，店裡有許多東西都不見了。

- **have the Midas touch**：to have the ability to make money easily (King Midas turned everything that he touched into gold) 點石成金（麥德斯國王能將所所有觸摸到的東西變成黃金）

  My uncle **has the Midas touch** and every business that he starts makes a lot of money.

  我叔叔有點石成金的力量，他所開始的每個事業都賺錢。

- **(not) have two cents to rub together**：to not have much money 沒錢

  My friend does **not have two cents to rub together** and he is always broke.

  我朋友沒錢，他總是哭窮告急。

金錢相關片語 (Money Idioms)

- **he who pays the piper calls the tune**：the person who pays for something has control over how the money is used 付錢的是老大

  He who pays the piper calls the tune and the owner of the sports team can decide who will play on the team.

  付錢的是老大，球隊老闆能決定誰上場誰坐板凳。

- **head over heels in debt**：to be deeply in debt 深陷債務中

  My cousin is **head over heels in debt** and has no money at all.

  我表哥深陷債務中，他一點錢都沒有。

- **heads or tails**：the face of a coin or the other side of the coin 錢幣的正反面；以拋錢幣的方式來解決事情

  The referee threw the coin to see if it would be **heads or tails** to decide which side gets to kick the ball.

  裁判用拋錢幣的方式來做決定哪一隊有發球權。

- **highway robber**：the charging of a high price for something 敲竹槓；打秋風

  The amount of money that the company is charging for its services is **highway robbery**.

  這間公司在服務上的收費簡直是敲竹槓。

- **hit the jackpot**：to make a lot of money suddenly (usually from gambling) 獲得累積的賭注 [獎金]；突然發大財

  We **hit the jackpot** at the casino and came home with much money.

  我們在賭場發大財帶了許多錢回家。

金錢相關片語 (Money Idioms)

- **honor (someone's) check**：to accept someone's personal check 承兌私人支票

  The bank refused to **honor** my **check** for the rent.
  銀行拒絕兌換我用來付房租的支票。

- **ill-gotten gains**：money acquired in dishonest or illegal manner 非法所得

  The **ill-gotten gains** of the politician were the subject of a large government inquiry.
  政治人物的非法所得是政府大規模調查的主題。

- **in clover**：in a very good financial situation 安逸奢侈

  My aunt and uncle have been living **in clover** since my uncle got his new job.
  自從我叔叔獲得新工作後，我叔叔和嬸嬸就一直過安逸奢侈的日子。

- **in debt**：owing money 負債

  The man is **in debt** and owes much money to many people.
  這個人在負債中而且還欠了很多人很多錢。

- **in kind**：in goods rather than money 實物

  I paid for the work on my car **in kind** rather than with cash.
  我以實物而非金錢來支付我汽車修理費用。

- **in the black**：to be profitable, to make money 有盈餘，賺錢

  Our company has been **in the black** since it started.
  我們公司從一開始就賺錢。

金錢相關片語 (Money Idioms)

- **in the chips**：with much money, wealthy 有錢

  My grandfather was **in the chips** after he discovered oil on his farm.
  我祖父在他農場上發現石油後就變得很有錢。

- **in the hole**：to be in debt, to owe money 欠債，有赤字

  I think that we are now **in the hole** and our business is having trouble.
  我覺得我們現在有赤字且營業上也有問題。

- **in the money**：to be wealthy, to suddenly get a lot of money 有的是錢，發大財

  I am **in the money** now that I won the lottery.
  我贏得樂透發大財了。

- **in the red**：to be unprofitable, to be losing money, to be in debt 赤字，賠錢，虧損

  The company has been **in the red** for several months now and may soon go bankrupt.
  公司近幾個月都赤字連連可能很快就要破產。

- **jack up the price (of something)**：to raise the price of something 抬高價錢

  The store **jacked up the price** of their summer stock at the beginning of the summer.
  這間商店在夏天一開始就調高夏日商品存貨的價錢。

金錢相關片語 (Money Idioms)

- **keep books**：to keep record of money that is earned and spent 記帳

  Our accountant is **keeping** careful **books** of all the transactions in the company.

  我們公司的會計仔細的記載所有交易的紀錄。

- **keep the wolf from the door**：to earn enough money to maintain oneself at a minimal level of existence 使不受飢寒

  My job does not pay very well but it is enough to **keep the wolf from the door**.

  我的工作待遇不好但足以供我溫飽。

- **kickback**：money paid illegally for favorable treatment 回扣

  The politician received several illegal **kickbacks** and was forced to resign.

  政治人物因接受回扣而被迫辭職。

- **last of the big spenders**：a humorous way to describe someone who spends a lot of money for something (although he or she may not want to spend it) 大手筆；百萬刷手（詼諧用法）

  The man is pretending to be the **last of the big spenders** as he spends money during his holidays.

  這人在假期時大手筆花錢。

- **lay away money**：to save money 存錢

  I am trying to **lay away money** to buy a car.

  我正在試著存錢買車。

金錢相關片語 (Money Idioms)

- **lay out (money)**：to spend or pay money 花錢

  I had to **lay out** a lot of **money** to get my car fixed so now I don't have much money.

  我得在修車上花很多錢所以我現在沒什麼錢。

- **layaway plan**：a plan in which one pays some money as a down payment and then pays a little more when one is able and store holds the goods until the full price is paid 先付訂金待餘款付清後再取貨的作法

  We bought our furniture on a **layaway plan** at the store.

  我們用先付訂金後付餘款再取貨的方法買家具。

- **let the buyer beware**：let the person who buys something check to see if the product is in good condition or has no problem 確定貨品無誤

  Consumers of electronic products should remember the motto of "**let the buyer beware**" when they buy something.

  購買電子產品的消費者要牢記「商品確定無誤」的格言。

- **live beyond one's means**：to spend more money than you can earn 寅吃卯糧

  The girl is **living beyond her means** and will soon have some serious financial problems.

  這女孩寅吃卯糧，她很快就會有財務問題。

- **live from hand to mouth**：to live on little money 僅夠餬口

  My friend has been **living from hand to mouth** and is now on welfare.

  我朋友一直是勉強餬口，他現在靠社會福利金過日子。

金錢相關片語 (Money Idioms)

- **live high off [on the hog]**：to have the best of everything, to live in great comfor
  養尊處優

  Jack has been **living high off** since he won the lottery.

  傑克贏得樂透後就過著養尊處優的日子。

- **live within one's means**：to spend no more money than one has 量入為出

  I try very hard to **live within my means** so that I do not have any financial pressure.

  我努力量入為出為的是不要有財務壓力。

- **be loaded**：to have lots of money; drunk, drunken 荷包滿滿；喝醉

  He **is loaded**; no wonder he can buy anything he wants.

  他很有錢，難怪他能買任何他想要的東西。

- **look like a million dollars**：to look very good 意氣飛揚

  The woman **looked like a million dollars** when she went to accept the award.

  這位女士領獎時看起來意氣飛揚。

- **make [lose] money hand over fist**：to lose money fast and in large amounts 怏
  速賺錢 [失財]

  The new coffee shop is **losing money hand over fist**.

  這間新咖啡店賠錢賠得很快。

金錢相關片語 (Money Idioms)

○ **lost one's shirt**：to lose all or most of one's money 賠光

> I **lost my shirt** in a small business and now I have no money.
>
> 我做小生意賠光了錢，現在我沒錢了。

○ **(not) made of money**：to not have a lot of money (usually used in the negative to say that you do not have enough money for something) 不是錢做的（通常有反諷意味，尤其是沒錢買東西時）

> I am **not made of money** and I do not like wasting it on stupid things.
>
> 我不是錢做的；我可不要把錢花在無聊的東西上。

○ **make a bundle [pile]**：to make a lot of money 賺大錢

> I **made a bundle** on the stock market and decided to buy a house.
>
> 我在股票市場上賺大錢，所以我決定買棟房子。

○ **make a check out to (someone)**：to write a check with someone's name on it 開支票給某人

> I **made a check out to** the man who repaired my bathroom.
>
> 我開支票給替我修浴室的人。

○ **make a fast [quick] buck**：to make money with little effort 賺輕鬆錢

> The young man is very lazy and he is always trying to **make a fast buck**.
>
> 這年輕人很懶，他總是想賺輕鬆錢。

M

金錢相關片語 (Money Idioms)

- **make a killing**：to make a large amount of money 發大財

  My sister **made a killing** when she worked overseas in the oil industry.

  我姊姊在替海外石油業工作時賺了大錢。

- **make a living**：to earn enough money to live 謀生

  The man works hard to **make a living** and support his family.

  這個人努力工作來養家活口。

- **make ends meet**：to have enough money to pay one's bills and other expenses 收支平衡

  I have been having trouble **making ends meet** because the rent for my apartment is very high.

  因為房租太高，我一直很難收支平衡。

- **make good money**：to earn a large amount of money 賺錢

  My friend **makes good money** at his new job.

  我朋友在新工作上賺了錢。

- **money burns a hole in (someone's) pocket**：someone spends money very quickly, someone is stimulated to spend money quickly 守不住錢

  The **money is burning a hole in** my **pocket** and I want to spend it.

  錢把我口袋燒了個洞；我要去花錢。

金錢相關片語 (Money Idioms)

- **money doesn't grow on trees**：money is valuable and shouldn't be wasted 錢不是樹上長的；金錢得來不易

  Money doesn't grow on trees and it is necessary to work hard and manage it well.

  金銀得來不易；要努力去賺還要好好管理。

- **money is no object**：it does not matter how much something costs 錢不是問題

  Money is no object and I plan to stay at the best hotels during my holiday.

  錢不是問題，我打算在假期中住最好的旅館。

- **(one's) money is on (someone)**：you think that someone will win a competition or sports event, etc. 把錢押在某人身上

  My money is on the young horse that is racing for the first time today.

  我把錢都押在今天第一次出賽的那匹幼馬上。

- **money is the root of all evil**：money causes most problems or wrongdoings in life 錢是罪惡的淵藪

  Many people believe that **money is the root of all evil** and that it causes people many problems.

  很多人都相信錢是罪惡的淵藪而錢也為人招致很多問題。

M

金錢相關片語 (Money Idioms)

- **money talks**：money gives one the power to get or do what he or she wants 有錢能使鬼推磨

  > **Money talks** and when I go to a restaurant with my rich friend we always get very good service.
  >
  > 有錢能使鬼推磨；我和我有錢的朋友去餐廳時總能得到非常好的服務。

- **nest egg**：the money that someone has saved up 存款

  > I made a **nest egg** when I was working and I am now able to go to school.
  >
  > 我在工作時存了些錢，所以我現在可以去學校上課。

- **nickel and dime (someone)**：to charge many small amount of money (which eventually equal a large amount of money) 小錢變大錢

  > The small repairs on my car are beginning to **nickel and dime** me.
  >
  > 我在修車上花的小錢已經越積越多了。

- **not for love nor money**：not for anything (no matter what the amount or price) 付錢免費都不要；無論如何

  > I will **not** meet with that woman again **for love or money**.
  >
  > 無論如何我都不要再和那女子見面。

- **on a dime**：in a very small space 狹窄的空間

  > I had to turn my car **on a dime** space after I entered the parking lot.
  >
  > 我進入停車場後必須在很窄的空間迴車。

金錢相關片語 (Money Idioms)

- **on a shoestring**：with a little money to spend, on a very low budget 預算緊，錢不夠

  My friend started his business **on a shoestring** but now it is very successful.
  我朋友的生意開始時錢很緊現在則變得非常成功。

- **on sale**：for sale at a discount price 拍賣

  The DVDs were **on sale** when I bought them.
  我是在大拍賣時買了這些DVD。

- **on the house**：paid by the owner of a business 老闆請客

  All of the drinks at the restaurant were **on the house**.
  餐廳裡所有的飲料都是老闆請客。

- **on the money**：exactly the right place or time or amount of something, exactly the right idea 正好，正是

  Our estimate of next year's budget is right **on the money**.
  我們對明年預算的預估是正確的。

- **on the take**：to be accepting bribes 收賄

  The agent at the border crossing seems to be **on the take**.
  戍守邊界的警衛好像收賄。

O

金錢相關片語 (Money Idioms)

- **pad the bill**：to add false expenses to a bill 浮報開銷

  The plumber who was fixing our plumbing system was **padding the bill** so we got a new plumber.

  水電工在修理時浮報開銷，所以我們換人了。

- **pass the buck**：to make another person decide something, to put the responsibility or blame on someone else 推諉責任

  Stop **passing the buck**! Someone has to take on the responsibility.

  別再推卸責任；總有人要負責任。

- **pass the hat**：to collect money for something (sometimes by passing a hat around to put the money into it) 募錢

  We **passed the hat** to collect some money for the homeless.

  我們為遊民募錢。

- **pay a king's ransom (for something)**：to pay a great deal of money for something 付出天價

  I had to **pay a king's ransom** for a ticket to the final baseball game.

  我得為最後一場棒球賽的門票付出天價。

- **pay an arm and a leg for (something)**：to pay a high price for something 付出很高代價

  I **paid an arm and a leg for** my car but I am not very happy with it.

  我為了我的車付出高價但我對它並不滿意。

金錢相關片語 (Money Idioms)

- **pay as you go**：to pay for things as they occur (rather than on credit) 付現不賒帳

  I will have to **pay as I go** if I go to graduate school next year.
  如果明年我要讀研究所的話，我就要付現金了。

- **pay in advance**：to pay for something before you get or use it 預付

  I must **pay in advance** for the courier service to deliver my boxes.
  如果要貨運公司運送箱子的話，我得先付錢。

- **pay off (someone)/pay (someone) off**：to pay someone a bribe or something 給錢行賄

  The owner of the store had to **pay off** the gang who were threatening him.
  商店老闆必須要付錢給威脅他的幫派分子。

- **pay off (something) /pay (something) off**：to pay the total amount of something 付清

  I **paid off** my student loan after one year.
  我一年就付清我的學生貸款。

- **pay one's way**：to pay the cost for something yourself 付自己的帳

  The young girl **paid her way** through college.
  這女孩自己付自己大學的費用。

金錢相關片語 (Money Idioms)

- **pay the piper**：to face the result of one's action, to receive punishment for something 承擔後果

  > I was forced to **pay the piper** when I realized that I had been late with my university essay.
  > 當我知道我的論文遲交時，我只好承擔後果。

- **pay through the nose**：to pay a very high price, to pay too much 所費不貲

  > I **paid through the nose** when I had to buy things I needed in a small town.
  > 我在一個小鎮為我需要買的東西付出高價。

- **pay up**：to pay now 馬上付款

  > I had to **pay up** my parking tickets or I would lose my driving license.
  > 我必須付清違規停車罰單否則我就會被吊銷駕照。

- **payoff**：a bribe 賄賂

  > The mayor received a **payoff** and was forced to resign from his position.
  > 市長因收賄而被迫辭掉市長職務。

- **pennies from heaven**：money that you do not expect to get 天降橫財

  > The money that I received from the government was like **pennies from heaven** and I was very happy.
  > 我很高興收到政府的錢；真是天降橫財。

P

金錢相關片語 (Money Idioms)

penny for one's thought：a request that ask someone what he or she is thinking about 問人在想什麼

> "I will give you a **penny for your thought**," I said to my friend who was looking out of the window.
>
> 我對往窗外看的朋友說：「你在想什麼？」

a penny saved is a penny earned：saving money by not spending it is the same as earning money from working 能省則省

> **A penny saved is a penny earned** and it is better to be thrifty sometimes than to only work more hours.
>
> 能省則省；有時節儉比加班賺錢還要好。

piggy bank：a small bank or container for saving money that is sometimes in the shape of a pig 存錢筒

> The small boy saved much money in his **piggy bank**.
>
> 小男孩存錢筒裡存了很多錢。

pinch pennies：to be careful with money, to be thrifty 摳門

> My grandmother always **pinches pennies** and never spends her money foolishly.
>
> 我奶奶總是很摳門，她從來不亂花錢。

P

金錢相關片語 (Money Idioms)

- **play the market**：to invest in the stock market 進場玩股票

  My father likes to **play the market** and he sometimes makes a lot of money.

  我父親喜歡進場玩股票，有時他能賺很多錢。

- **pony up**：to pay 付錢

  I had to **pony up** a lot of money to get my car repaired.

  我為修車付了很多錢。

- **pour money down the drain**：to waste money 浪費錢

  The man is **pouring money down the drain** by always repairing his old car.

  這個人老是修他的舊車，為此他浪費了很多錢。

- **put in one's two cents (worth)**：to add one's comment or opinion to a discussion 表示意見

  I stood up in the meeting and **put in my two cent worth** before I sat down.

  我在會議中坐下前先站起來發表意見。

- **put one's money where one's mouth is**：to stop talking about something and do it, to stop talking and make a bet on something 多說無益

  I was forced to **put my money where my mouth is** an either go to Europe or stop talking about it.

  我被迫要不就去歐洲要不就閉嘴。

金錢相關片語 (Money Idioms)

put the bite on (someone)：to try to get money from someone 向人借錢或敲竹槓

The young man often **puts the bite on** his father before the weekend.
這年輕人總是在週末前向他父親要錢。

quick buck：some money earned easily and quickly 輕鬆錢

The small company is only interested in making a **quick buck** and is not interested in product quality.
這公司只在乎賺輕鬆錢而不在意產品品質。

quote a price：to say in advance how much something will cost 報價

I asked the salesman to **quote a price** for the new product.
我要求業務員對新產品報價。

rain check：a promise to repeat an invitation at a later date 改日的邀請

I decided to take a **rain check** and will go to the restaurant with my friend another day.
我決定延緩和朋友進餐的邀請。

raise an ante：to increase your demands or the amount that you spend for something 抬高賭注

The union **raised the ante** with the company when they said that they were going to go on strike.
工會用罷工來抬高和公司抗爭的賭注。

R

金錢相關片語 (Money Idioms)

rake in the money：to make a lot of money 賺大錢

> We have been **raking in the money** at our restaurant since it opened.
> 我們餐廳自開幕起就賺大錢。

rake off (some money)/rake (some money) off：to steal a portion of a payment or money 中飽私囊

> The cashier was **raking off** some of the money from the store.
> 商店收銀員中飽私囊。

red cent：a small sum of money (usually used in the negative) 一文不值

> I would not give a **red cent** for my neighbor's car.
> 我不會為我鄰居的車付任何錢。

roll in money：to have lots of money 錢很多

> The man is **rolling in money** and he always has much money to spend.
> 這人很有錢，他總是有很多錢可用。

salt away (money) /salt (money) away：to save money 藏錢

> The old man **salted away** thousands of dollars before he died.
> 老人在死前藏了不少錢。

save up (for something)：to save money in order to buy something 存錢

> I am **saving up for** a new television set.
> 我為買新電視機存錢。

R

金錢相關片語 (Money Idioms)

- **scrape (something) together/scrape together (something)** : to save small amounts of money (usually with some difficulty) for something 湊錢

  We **scraped together** some money and bought a present for our friend.

  我們湊錢買禮物給朋友。

- **scrimp and save** : to spend little money in order to save for something 節省

  The woman has been **scrimping and saving** for her son's education.

  這女子一直為她兒子的教育省吃儉用。

- **see the color of (someone's) money** : to make sure that someone has enough money for something 讓人付錢

  I will not give the man the new product until I **see the color of his money**.

  沒看到他的錢我是不會給他新產品的。

- **set (someone) back/set back (someone)** : to cost certain amount of money 破費

  My friend asked me how much my new coat had **set me back**.

  我朋友問我為新外套花了多少錢。

- **shake (someone) down/shake down (someone)** : to blackmail or extract money from someone 勒索某人

  The gang tried to **shake down** the owner of the small store.

  幫派分子試著勒索小店老闆。

S

金錢相關片語 (Money Idioms)

- **shell out (money)/shell (money) out**：to pay money for something 付錢

  My father **shelled out** a lot of money to get our house painted.

  我父親為了粉刷房子付了很多錢。

- **sitting on a goldmine**：to own something very valuable (and often not realize this) 坐擁金山

  The child is **sitting on a goldmine** with his collection of rare stamps.

  這小孩因收藏稀有郵票而坐擁金山。

- **smart money is on (someone or something)**：people who know about money or business think that someone or something is good 值得投資的人或事物；正確的選擇

  The **smart money is on** the government to introduce the new law this week.

  政府本週宣布新法律是件十拿九穩的事。

- **sock away (some money or something) /sock (some money or something) away**：to save or store some money or something 把錢留在一邊

  I am trying to **sock away** some money for my holiday.

  我正試著為假期留些錢。

- **splurge on (something)**：to spend money fast and in large amounts 亂花錢

  We decided to **splurge** and go to a nice restaurant for dinner.

  我們決定奢侈一點去家好餐廳吃晚餐。

S

金錢相關片語 (Money Idioms)

- **square accounts with (someone)**：to settle one's financial account with someone 結清帳務

  > I went to the small store to **square accounts with** its owner.
  > 我到小店和老闆結清帳務。

- **squirrel away (some money)/squirrel (some money) away**：to save some money 留些錢

  > I was able to **squirrel away** much money from my previous job.
  > 我能在上個工作存些錢。

- **stone broke**：to have no money 一點錢也沒有

  > My friend is usually **stone broke** before the pay day.
  > 我朋友通常在發薪日前都會一點錢都沒剩。

- **strapped for cash**：to have little or no money 為缺現金所困

  > I am **strapped for cash** at the moment so I will not be able to go on a holiday.
  > 我現在沒錢所以無法去度假。

- **strike gold**：to find or do something that makes you rich 挖到金礦發了財

  > The company was able to **strike gold** with their new product.
  > 公司因新產品而發了財。

S

金錢相關片語 (Money Idioms)

strike it rich：to suddenly become rich or successful 一步登天

> My grandfather **struck it rich** when he was young but when he died he had no money.
>
> 我祖父年輕時因發財而一步登天，但他死時則是一貧如洗。

take a beating：to lose money 失利，賠錢

> My friend **took a beating** on the stock market and he has now stopped buying stocks.
>
> 我朋友在股票市場上賠錢，他現在已經停止買賣了。

take the money and run：to accept what is offered to you before the offer is gone 見好就收

> I plan to **take the money and run** as I do not believe that I will get any more money for the settlement of my car accident.
>
> 我決定見好就收，因為我不覺得我可以在車禍中得到更多好處。

take up a collection：to collect money for something 捐獻

> We plan to **take up a collection** for the wife of the dead manager.
>
> 我們計畫為過世經理的太太發起捐款。

T

金錢相關片語 (Money Idioms)

- **throw good money after bad**：to waste additional money after already wasting money on the same thing 反覆在同樣事情上浪費錢

  I do not want to **throw good money after bad** so I will not pay any more money to fix my car.

  我不要在我車上浪費了錢，所以我不會再花一毛錢修車。

- **throw money around**：to spend a lot of money without worrying if you are wasting it 肆無忌憚地花錢

  The government is **throwing** much **money around** as they prepare for the large exhibition.

  政府在準備大型展覽上肆無忌憚地花錢。

- **throw money at (something)**：to spend a lot of money for a project or something without thinking about how the money should be spent 亂花錢

  The city is **throwing** a lot of **money at** the project to fix the stadium roof.

  市政府在修理體育館屋頂上亂花錢。

- **tidy sum of money**：a rather large amount of money 一筆可觀的錢

  I was able to get a **tidy sum of money** from my grandmother as an inheritance.

  我從我祖母處得到一筆可觀的遺產。

- **tighten one's belt**：to live on less money than usual 勒緊褲帶

  We decided to **tighten our belt** and try to save up some money for the future.

  我們決定勒緊褲帶並為未來存錢。

T

金錢相關片語 (Money Idioms)

- **tightfisted (with money)**：to be very stingy with money 吝嗇

  My uncle is very **tightfisted with money** and does not want to spend any at all.
  我叔叔很吝嗇一點錢也不花。

- **time is money**：time is valuable so do not waste it 時間就是金錢

  Time is money and I do not want to waste time talking to our supervisor because she always wants to argue with me.
  時間就是金錢；我不要把時間花在和老是喜歡和我拌嘴的主管的談話上。

- **(not) worth a cent [dime, a red cent, a plugged nickel, two cents]**：does (not) have some (any) real value 不值一文錢

  The antique desk is **not worth a dime** although everybody thinks it is very valuable.
  儘管大家以為這張骨董書桌很有價值，實際上它一文不值。

- **worth its weight in gold**：to be very valuable 很有價值

  The new secretary is very smart and she is **worth her weight in gold**.
  這位新祕書很聰明，她是個極有價值的人。

- **worth one's salt**：to be worth what one is paid 物值所值

  Our secretary is **worth her salt** and is a great asset to our company.
  我們的祕書值得我們付給她的每分錢，她是公司重要的資產。

W

測驗題 (Idiom Quizzes)

Choose an idiom to replace the expression in the blankets:

1. My sister's husband is (in good financial condition) after many financial problems last year.

   A cooking the books   B betting his bottom dollar   C back on his feet
   D bringing home the bacon

2. I spent my (last small amount of money) on the ticket for the basketball game.

   A bottom dollar   B cold hard cash   C money to burn   D kickback

3. My father worked hard all of his life (earning the family living).

   A passing the buck   B paying through the nose   C stone broke   D bringing home the bacon

4. I decided to (sell all of my belongings) and go and work overseas.

   A strike it rich   B cash in my chips   C put in my two cents   D tighten my belt

5. I was (out of money) at the supermarket and I could not pay for my groceries.

   A pinching pennies   B padding the bill   C caught short   D paying away money

測驗題 (Idiom Quizzes)

6. Everybody in our class (contributed) some money for the New Year's party.

   A cleaned up   B cashed in   C salted away   D chipped in

7. You can often buy used pocket books for (a very cheap price).

   A a dime a dozen   B an arm and a leg   C pay dirt   D a piggy bank

8. I was (without money) many times when I first started working.

   A raking in the money   B worth my salt   C laying away money   D flat broke

9. My neighbor seems to be (short of money) at the moment.

   A loaded   B deadbeat   C hard up   D in the black

10. Our company has been (losing money) for over three years now.

   A making a killing   B in the red   C on a dime   D putting in their two cents worth

11. My friend made (a lot of money) when he was working in the oil industry.

   A a bundle   B ends meet   C a piggy bank   D a living

12. We were able to buy the house (very cheap) so we decided to try to buy it immediately.

  A worth our salt   B stone broke   C for a song   D on a dime

13. My sister went to Las Vegas and (won a lot of money) at the casino.

  A made ends meet   B lost her shirt   C greased her palm   D hit the jackpot

14. The woman with the three children is having a difficult time to (pay her bills).

  A make ends meet   B bet her bottom dollar   C feel like a million bucks
  D make a bundle

15. The man is (very rich) but he never likes to spend his money.

  A cut-rate   B loaded   C cooking the books   D in the whole

16. The company president received (some illegal money) from the contractor who wanted to get building contract.

  A a red cent   B a quick buck   C a kickback   D a rain check

17. My father (lost most of his money) on the stock market.

  A burnt a hole in his pocket   B lost his shirt   C picked up the tab   D padded the bill

18. The family has (more money than they need) so they often go on a nice holiday.

   A cold hard cash   B chicken feed   C bet on the wrong horse   D money to burn

19. The drinks were (paid for by the owner) as it was the tenth anniversary of the restaurant.

   A on the house   B on a shoestring   C strapped for cash   D penny wise and pound foolish

20. My sister and her husband paid (much money) for their house.

   A on a shoestring   B a rain check   C an arm and a leg   D in kind

21. I had to (pay) some money for the health club fees when I joined the club.

   A pony up   B break even   C pay off   D salt away

22. The woman is always (very careful with her money) and keeps a very strict budget.

   A worth her salt   B padding the bill   C putting in her two cents   D pinching pennies

23. My friend asked me how much my new car had (cost).

   A taken a beating   B picked up the tab   C made ends meet   D set me back

測驗題 (Idiom Quizzes)

24.I tried hard to give my (opinion) but I was unable to do so.

A gravy train   B layaway plan   C two cents worth   D cheapskate

25.I had to (live on less money than usual) after I quit my part-time job.

A break even   B tighten my belt   C ante up   D make money hand over fist

解答 (Answer Keys)

1. C	2. A	3. D	D. B	5. C
6. D	7. A	8. D	9. C	10. B
11. A	12. C	13. D	14. A	15. B
16. C	17. B	18. D	19. A	20. C
21. D	22. C	23. D	24. C	25. B

Number Idioms

數字遊戲

數字遊戲 (Number Idioms)

all-in-one：combined, all the necessary features of something in one unit 所有功能集一身

> Many DVD players have a recording and playing function **all-in-one**.
> 很多影音光碟機都能集錄影、播放於一身。

all in one breath：spoken rapidly while one is very excited 一口氣地

> I told my friend about the accident **all in one breath**.
> 我一口氣把整個意外告訴我朋友。

all in one piece：safely, without damage 安然無恙

> The piano arrived at its destination **all in one piece**.
> 鋼琴安然無恙地送達目的地。

all rolled in one：combined in one person or thing 一體

> The man is president and vice-president **all rolled in one**.
> 這個人身兼總經理和副總經理於一身。

as busy as one-armed paperhanger：very busy 非常忙碌

> I was as busy **as a one-armed paperhanger** during the last two weeks.
> 我在過去兩個星期非常忙碌。

as one：as if a group were one person 一致

> The crowd stood **as one** and began to cheer during the game.
> 群眾在球賽中一致地歡呼。

數字遊戲 (Number Idioms)

- **as phony as a three-dollar bill**：phony, not genuine 假的

  The woman's excuses are **as phony as a three-dollar bill** and I do not believe any of them.

  那女子的藉口很假，我一個也不相信。

- **at first**：initially, at the beginning 一開始

  At first we had no plans for the weekend but later we decided to go to a movie.

  一開始我們對週末沒計畫但後來我們決定去看電影。

- **at one time**：at a time in the past 曾經

  At one time the man had no money but now he is very rich.

  這人曾經窮過但現在卻很富有。

- **at one with (someone)**：to share the same view as others, to be in agreement with others 一致；協力

  The members of the committee are **at one with** me over my decision to cancel the meeting.

  委員會成員對取消會議的看法和我的決定一致。

- **at sixes and sevens**：in a state of confusion 亂七八糟

  The workers were **at sixes and sevens** after the company announced that it was going out of business.

  工人在公司宣布歇業時顯得非常混亂。

數字遊戲 (Number Idioms)

at the eleventh hour：at the last possible moment 在最後一刻

> **At the eleventh hour** the city and the garbage collectors settled their contract dispute.
>
> 市政府和垃圾收集工人在最後一刻就有爭議的合約達成協議。

back to square one：back to where one started 回到起點

> We were forced to go **back to square one** in our efforts to change the name of the company.
>
> 我們在改變公司名稱的努力上又回到原點。

bat a thousand：to be extremely successfully at something 高打擊；非常成功

> Recently, I have been **batting a thousand** in my attempts to sell the new product.
>
> 最近我在銷售新產品上百戰百勝。

by the dozen：twelve at a time, in a group of twelve; many, by a large number 一打；很多

> The children were eating the donuts **by the dozen**.
>
> 孩子們吃了很多的甜甜圈。
>
> The fans come **by the dozen** to see the famous athlete.
>
> 很多運動迷來看這位有名的運動員。

cast the first stone：to be the first one to criticize or attack someone 率先攻擊或批評

> I told my friend that he should be careful not to **cast the first stone** in an argument.
>
> 我告訴我朋友他該小心千萬別在爭論時率先攻擊。

數字遊戲 (Number Idioms)

- **catch forty winks**：to take a nap, to get some sleep 小睡

  I drove all night until I was very tired so I stopped to **catch forty winks**.
  我整夜開車直到我累到要小睡一會兒才停。

- **cut both [two] ways**：to be capable of having two opposite effects, to produce advantages and disadvantages 利弊正反好壞並陳

  The decision by the company **cut both ways**. Some people were happy while others were not.
  公司的決定使得幾家歡樂幾家愁。

- **deep-six (someone or something)**：to get rid of or dispose of someone or something 解決；處理

  I decided to **deep-six** some of the old comics that I had collected.
  我決定處理掉我所收集的舊漫畫。

- **a dime a dozen**：cheap and common, lots of something 便宜貨

  Used paperback books are **a dime a dozen** at the used bookstore.
  二手書在舊書店裡是便宜貨。

- **divide (something) fifty-fifty**：to divide something into two equal parts 平分，均分

  We decided to **divide** the money that we earned **fifty-fifty**.
  我們決定平分所賺到的錢。

數字遊戲 (Number Idioms)

- **do a number on (someone or something)**：to damage or harm someone or something 計算，陷害，動手腳

  > The young man **did a number on** the car that he borrowed from his uncle.
  > 年輕人在向他叔叔借的車子上動了手腳。

- **do (someone) one better**：to do something superior to what someone else has done 勝人一籌

  > I decided to **do** my friend **one better** and volunteer for three weeks rather than two weeks.
  > 我決定勝過我朋友所以我當三週志工而非兩個星期。

- **dressed to the nines**：to be dressed in one's best clothes 盛裝

  > The woman at the party was **dressed to the nines**.
  > 這女子盛裝出席聚會。

- **eleventh-hour decision**：a decision that is made at the last possible minute 最後關頭所做出的決議

  > The sport's federation made an **eleventh-hour decision** to suspend the star player.
  > 運動協會在最後關頭做出禁止明星球員出賽的決議。

- **every once in a while**：occasionally, infrequently 偶爾

  > **Every once in a while** I play tennis with my friend.
  > 我偶爾和我朋友打網球。

數字遊戲 (Number Idioms)

(I, you, he) for one：as one example, even if the only one 以⋯來說

> **I for one**, do not believe that our boss will change the company policy about new staff.
>
> 就我來說，我不相信公司老闆會改變對新進員工的政策。

for one thing：for one reason (among others) 舉例；就⋯而言

> It is not possible to use the old building. **For one thing**, it will never pass the fire inspection.
>
> 使用老建築物不可能。舉例說，它一定無法通過消防檢查。

get (someone's) number：to find out someone's telephone number 找出某人電話

> I plan to **get the man's number** from one of his friends.
>
> 我決定從他朋友身上找到他的電話。

get the third degree：to be questioned in great detail about something 接受詳細查詢

> When the boy returned from school he **got the third degree** from his mother.
>
> 當男孩從學校回來後，他受到他母親嚴厲詳盡的查問。

give me five：hit someone with one's hand to show that one is happy about something 擊掌歡呼

> "**Give me five!**" I said after I scored a goal in the game.
>
> 我在射門得分後說：「讓我們擊掌歡呼！」

G

數字遊戲 (Number Idioms)

- **give three cheers for (someone)/give (someone) three cheers**：to give praise or approval to someone who has done well 為表現優異者歡呼

  > The crowd **gave three cheers for** the team after they won the title game.
  > 群眾在球隊贏得錦標賽後為球隊歡呼。

- **have one too many**：have too much alcohol to drink 喝多了酒

  > The man **had one too many** so his friends would not let him drive home.
  > 這人喝多了，所以他的朋友們不讓他開車回家。

- **have (someone's) number**：to get the key information to be able to understand someone 了解對方

  > I **have** that man's **number**. He is a liar and cannot be trusted.
  > 我知道那人的底細，他是個騙子不能相信他。

- **have two strikes against (someone)**：to have a number of things that are working against one which make success more difficult 再一次就出局或失敗

  > The man already **had two strikes against** him when he went to apply for the job.
  > 這人早在求職時就已經受到警告了。

- **hole in one**：a golf ball that Is hit into the hole with only one shot 一桿進洞；運氣非常好

  > Can you imagine Jack has pulled that deal off? **Hole in one!**
  > 你能相信傑克竟然在那筆交易中成功？運氣真好！

數字遊戲 (Number Idioms)

◉ **hundred and one**：very many 很多

> I can think of **hundred and one** reasons why the new employee is not capable of doing his job.
>
> 我能想出很多這名新職員不稱職的原因。

◉ **hundred to one chance [shot]**：a small chance that is not likely to bring success 成功機會渺然

> My friend only has a **hundred to one shot** at getting the job that he has applied for.
>
> 我朋友得到他所應徵工作的機會很渺然。

◉ **in one ear and out the other**：ignored, not listened to or not heard 左耳進右耳出；不在意或聽不進去

> The teacher told the students about their homework but it went **in one ear and out the other**.
>
> 老師告訴學生他們的作業，但沒人在聽。

◉ **in one fell [single] swoop**：in one incident, as one event 一舉，一下子

> **In one fell** swoop my friend got a new car, a new job and a new girlfriend.
>
> 我朋友一下子新車、新工作和新女朋友都有了。

◉ **in round numbers [figures]**：an estimated number, a number that has been rounded off to an easier or shorter number 大約的數字

> The mechanic told us **in round figures** how much it will cost to fix our car.
>
> 技工告訴我們修車的大約費用。

數字遊戲 (Number Idioms)

- **in two minds about (something)**：to be undecided about something 三心二意

  > My niece is **in two minds about** whether or not she should visit her father in the U.S. this summer.
  > 我姪女對是否在今年夏天去美國探視她父親一事三心二意。

- **in two shakes of a lamb's tail**：very quickly 很快地

  > Wait one minute. I will help you **in two shakes of a lamb's tail**.
  > 等我一下。我很快就會幫你。

- **it takes two to tango**：if a problem or argument involve two people then both people are responsible for the problem 一個巴掌拍不響

  > **It takes two to tango** and my friend should not blame me for all the problems.
  > 一個巴掌拍不響；我朋友不該把問題的責任都怪在我身上。

- **kill two birds with one stone**：to achieve two aims with one effort or action 一舉兩得

  > By canceling the project, the construction company **kills two birds with one stone**.
  > 建設公司取消興建計畫是件一舉兩得的事。

- **know the trick or two**：to know a special way to deal with a problem 知曉個中三昧

  > My father **knows a trick or two** about how to make money in the stock market.
  > 我父親對如何在股票市場中賺錢頗有心得。

數字遊戲 (Number Idioms)

lesser of the two evils：the smaller of the two things, the one with least amount 較小的，次要的

I did not want to take the job but it was the **lesser of the two evils** because having no job was even worse.

我本不想要這個工作，但和沒工作比我還是要了。

like two peas in a pod：very close or intimate, very similar 酷似，一模一樣

The two girls are **like tow peas in a pod** and are very good friends.

這兩個女孩長得很像而且她們是好朋友。

look after number one：to only look after or think about oneself 自私自利

My neighbor only **looks after number one** and he will not help other people.

我鄰居只為自己想，他絕不會幫助他人。

million and one：very many 很多

There was a **million and one** things to do at the festival.

在節慶時有很多事要做。

million dollar question：an important but difficult question 重要且困難的問題

The **million dollar question** is whether we should buy a new computer or not.

重要的問題是我們到底要不要買部新電腦。

L

數字遊戲 (Number Idioms)

million miles away：to be not paying attention to something, to be distracted and daydreaming about something 神遊太虛

I was a **million miles away** and I did not hear anything that the teacher said.

我神遊太虛沒有聽見老師說的話。

nine-day wonder：someone or something that briefly attracts a lot of attention 一時的轟動

The man was a **nine-day wonder** and was soon forgotten by most people at his former company.

這人只不過是一時的轟動，他很快就被前一家公司的人所遺忘。

nine times out of ten：almost always 總是

Nine times out of ten a small computer problem can be easily fixed.

電腦的小問題總是很容易就被解決。

nine-to-five attitude：an attitude towards work where you do not do anything beyond the minimum that is required of you 只做分內事的態度

The man has a **nine-to-five attitude** and he is not doing well as a salesperson in his company.

這人只做該做的事，他在公司裡做一名業務員做的很糟糕。

nine-to-five job：a routine job in an office that involves standard office hours (usually 9:00 a.m. until 5:00 p.m.) 朝九晚五；固定時間的工作

My father always works at a **nine-to- five job**.

我父親總是做上下班固定時間的工作。

數字遊戲 (Number Idioms)

no two ways about (something)：no alternative, certain 只有一條路

The manager said that there are **no two ways about** it and the worker must improve or he will be fired.

經理說不是做好就是被開除；別無選擇。

not give two hoots about (someone or something)：does not care about someone or something a bit/at all 不理不甩

I do **not give tow hoots** if my friend comes to visit me or not.

我朋友來不來我無所謂。

not touch (someone or something) with a ten foot pole：to not want to involved with someone or something under any circumstances 敬鬼神而遠之

I would **not touch** the computer problem with a ten foot pole.

我對電腦問題總是敬鬼神而遠之。

a number of (things or people)：some things, some people 有些事，有些人

A number of people complained about the food in the new restaurant.

有些人抱怨新餐廳的菜。

on all fours：on one's hands and knees 手腳並用

The man was **on all fours** looking for his car keys.

這人手腳並用找他的車鑰匙。

N

數字遊戲 (Number Idioms)

on cloud nine：very happy about something 極樂之狀

> My sister has been **on cloud nine** since she won the money in the contest.
> 我的姊姊自從在競賽中贏得獎金後就一直處在非常快樂的境界。

on the one hand：from one point of view or opinion 從某個角度來看

> **On the one hand** I do not want to go to the conference, but on the other hand I really must go.
> 一方面我不想去參加研討會，但從另一個角度來看我一定得去。

one after another：one thing or person follow another 一個接著一個

> The customers came **one after another** to look at the new computer operating system.
> 顧客一個接著一個來參觀新的電腦操作系統。

one and all：everyone 所有人

> **One and all** were invited to the party.
> 所有人都被邀請去參加聚會。

one and only：the only person or thing, unique 獨一無二

> Our university has the **one and only** medical imaging system in the country.
> 我們的大學裡有全國獨一無二的醫學影像系統。

數字遊戲 (Number Idioms)

one and the same：exactly the same 完全一樣

> Doing my job at home or at the company is **one and the same** to me.
> 在我家或在公司做我的工作對我而言都一樣。

one at a time：individually 一次一個

> The children went to the front of the classroom **one at a time**.
> 孩子們一次一個到教室前面。

one by one：individually, one at a time 一個接一個

> The children entered the school building **one by one**.
> 孩子們一個接著一個進入學校大樓內。

one for the (record) books：a record-breaking act 創紀錄之舉

> The athlete's performance in the race was **one for the record books**.
> 這個運動員在比賽中的表現是創紀錄之舉。

one for the road：one last drink (usually alcohol) before one leaves for home 上路前最後一杯酒

> We decided to stay at the party and have **one for the road** before taking taxi home.
> 我們決定在搭計程車回家前待在派對上喝最後一杯。

數字遊戲 (Number Idioms)

- **one good man deserves another**：if someone helps you then you should help them in return 禮尚往來

  > **One good man deserves another** and I was happy to help my friend after he helped me.
  >
  > 我很高興在我朋友幫助我後能有機會幫助他，禮尚往來一下。

- **one [a] heck [hell] of a (someone or something)**：the emphasis that someone or something is very good or very bad at something 好傢伙（可好可壞）

  > The man is **a hell of a** [one] runner and he has won many races.
  >
  > 這人是個好跑者，他贏得很多比賽。

- **one in a hundred**：one among one hundred of something 百分之一

  > About **one in a hundred** of the products are defective.
  >
  > 產品大約每一百個中有一個是有瑕疵的。

- **one in a million**：unique, one of a very few 罕見

  > Our coach is **one in a million**. He is fantastic.
  >
  > 我們的教練相當罕見；他棒極了。

- **one in a thousand**：one out of one thousand 千分之一

  > The chance of getting the job is about **one in a thousand**.
  >
  > 得到工作的機會大概是千分之一。

數字遊戲 (Number Idioms)

- **one jump ahead of (someone or something)**：one step in advance of someone or something 比…搶先一步

  > My boss is always **one jump ahead of** the rest of the employees.
  > 我老闆總是在所有員工中搶先一步。

- **one man's meat is another man's poison**：something that one person likes may not be liked by another person 一人之藥可能是他人之毒

  > **One man's meat is another man's poison** and everybody dislikes the food that my friend likes.
  > 一個人喜歡而其他人討厭；只有我朋友喜歡那種大家都討厭的食品。

- **a one-night stand**：an activity that lasts only one night 只持續一夜的活動

  > The rock band played several **one-night stands** last month.
  > 這個搖滾樂團上個月有幾場只有一夜的演出。

- **one of the boys**：an accepted member of a group 自己人

  > Our boss tries to be **one of the boys** but actually nobody likes him.
  > 我老闆想和大家打成一片，但老實說沒人喜歡他。

- **one of these days**：soon, before long, someday 總有一天

  > **One of these days** they plan to open a new movie theater in our neighborhood.
  > 他們計畫將來在我們的社區裡開一家電影院。

O

數字遊戲 (Number Idioms)

- **one of those days**：a bad day where many things go wrong 倒楣的一天

  It was **one of those days** and from early morning this went wrong.
  真是倒楣的一天，一大早起事情就不對。

- **one of those things**：something is unfortunate but it must be accepted 不幸但又必須接受的事

  My friend's illness is **one of those things** and there is nothing we can do about it.
  我朋友的病就是不幸但卻無法不接受的事情，真讓我們束手無策。

- **one or two**：a few, a small number 少數

  There were only **one or two** people at the meeting so it was postponed.
  只有幾個人出席會議所以會議延期了。

- **one person's trash is another person's treasure**：something that one person considers of no value may be considered valuable by somebody else 某人眼中的垃圾是另一個人心目中的珍寶

  One persons' trash is another person's treasure and my friend likes to buy used good at the flea market.
  有人棄如敝屣而他人視為珍寶；我朋友就喜歡在跳蚤市場裡買舊貨。

- **one sandwich short of a picnic**：not very smart 不機靈

  The janitor is **one sandwich short of a picnic** and he makes many mistakes.
  管理員不靈光犯了許多錯誤。

數字遊戲 (Number Idioms)

- **the one that got away**：a fish that you did not catch, an opportunity that you missed 沒抓到的魚；沒把握到的機會

  My father has caught many fish but the biggest one is **the one that got away**.
  我父親捕到很多魚但最大的那隻總是逃脫掉的那隻。

- **one thing leads to another**：doing one thing or one event will set the stage of something else 一件事連帶引起另一件事

  One thing led to another and suddenly it was too late to catch the bus home.
  一件事連帶引起另一件事，突然連回家的巴士都錯過了。

- **one to a customer**：each person can received only one of something 一人一件

  The items were limited to **one to a customer**.
  這款物品限量一人一件。

- **one up on (someone)**：to have an advantage over someone 略勝一籌

  I am **one up on** my friend because he is still looking for a job while I have already found one.
  我比我朋友好一點；他還在找工作而我已經找到了。

- **one way or another**：somehow 反正

  One way or another I will phone my friend this evening.
  反正今晚我會打電話給我朋友。

O

數字遊戲 (Number Idioms)

- **one's days are numbered**：someone is facing death or dismissal from a job or something 來日不多

  The salesman has made many mistakes and **his days are numbered** in his job.

  業務員犯太多錯，他在工作上可說是來日不多。

- **one's lucky number comes up**：someone is lucky or has good fortune 運氣好

  My lucky number finally **came up** and I was chosen to go Los Angeles to represent our company at the conference.

  我走運了！我被選出代表公司出席在洛杉磯的大會。

- **one's opposite number**：someone who has the same position as oneself in another company or organization 與對方地位相等或相當者

  I spoke with **my opposite number** in the other company but we could not finalize the sale.

  我和對方公司職位相當的人通過電話，但仍無法做出決議。

- **put two and two together**：to make a correct guess, to figure something out from the information that you have 根據事實做出明顯的決定

  We were able to **put two and two together** and discovered who was sending the unwanted messages.

  我們根據事實發現是那個人在傳送沒必要的訊息。

數字遊戲 (Number Idioms)

in seventh heaven：a situation of great happiness 七重天；在無上幸福

> The woman has been **in seventh heaven** since she moved to the new apartment.
>
> 這女子自從搬到新公寓後就很快樂。

six feet under：dead and buried 入土為安

> My uncle has been **six feet under** for over five years now.
>
> 我叔叔入土為安已經五年多了。

six of one and half a dozen of the other：there is little difference between two things or situations 兩者相差無幾

> Whatever you do is no problem for me. It is **six of one and half a dozen of the other**.
>
> 你如何做我都無所謂；兩者沒甚麼差別。

sixth sense：a power to know or feel that things are beyond the five senses of sight/hearing/smell/taste/touch 第六感

> The woman has a **sixth sense** and she seems to know what other people are thinking.
>
> 這女子有第六感，她似乎知道其他人在想什麼。

stand on one's own two feet：to be independent and self-sufficient 獨立且自給自足

> The boy learned early to **stand on his own two feet**.
>
> 這男孩很小就學習要獨立且自給自足。

S

數字遊戲 (Number Idioms)

- **a stitch in time saves nine**：any damage or mistake should be corrected immediately in order to prevent it from becoming worse 及時行事，事半功倍

  > You should repair your car before it becomes worse. Remember, **a stitch in time saves nine**.
  >
  > 你應該在車子變得更糟前把它修好；別忘了：及時行事，事半功倍。

- **take five**：to take one brief (about five minutes) rest period 休息五分鐘

  > The city workers stopped to **take five** after working hard all morning.
  >
  > 市政府工人在辛苦工作一上午後暫時休息一下。

- **tell (someone) a thing or two (about something)**：to scold someone, to become angry at someone 指責

  > I plan to **tell** my neighbor **a thing or two** about his dog when I see him.
  >
  > 我決定在看見我鄰居時跟他埋怨他的狗。

- **ten to one**：very likely 很可能

  > **Ten to one** our secretary will come to work late again today.
  >
  > 今天我們的祕書很可能又會上班遲到。

- **that makes two of us**：the same thing is true for me 我有同感

  > A: I don't want to go to the meeting.
  >
  > 我不想去開會。
  >
  > B: **That makes two of us**.
  >
  > 我有同感。

數字遊戲 (Number Idioms)

- **think twice (before doing something)**：to consider carefully whether one should do something or not 三思而後行

  > I told my cousin to **think twice** before he decides to quit the job.
  > 我告訴我表哥在辭掉工作前要三思而後行。

- **a thousand and one**：very many 很多

  > I can think of **a thousand and one** reasons why I do not want to travel with you.
  > 我可以想出很多理由為何我不想和你一起旅行。

- **three sheets to the wind**：drunk 喝醉了

  > The man walked down the street with **three sheets to the wind**.
  > 這喝醉酒的人沿著街走下去。

- **two bricks shy of a load**：to be not very smart or clever 反應遲鈍

  > The man is **two bricks shy of a load** and he is very hard to deal with.
  > 這人很遲鈍，要和他相處很難。

- **two heads are better than one**：two people working together can achieve better results than one person working alone 兩個臭皮匠勝過一個諸葛亮

  > **Two heads are better than one** when you are trying to solve a difficult problem.
  > 在解決困難的問題時是兩個臭皮匠勝過一個諸葛亮。

T

數字遊戲 (Number Idioms)

- **two of a kind**：people or things that are of the same type or are similar in character or attitude, etc. 一丘之貉

  The boys are **two of a kind** and they love to spend time together.

  這些男孩是一夥的，他們喜歡花時間在一起。

- **two-time (someone)**：to cheat on one's partner by seeing someone else 劈腿

  The couple separated when the man began to **two-time** his wife.

  這對夫妻因先生劈腿而分手。

- **two wrongs don't make a right**：you cannot justify doing something wrong or bad just because someone else did the same thing to you 以其人之道還治其人未必是對的

  Two wrongs don't make a right and if someone does something bad you should not try and hurt them as well.

  一報還一報不對，你不能因為他人對不起你就去傷害他。

- **two's company, three's crowd**：two people (usually a couple on a date) are happier when nobody else is around 多一人就成電燈泡

  My friend wanted to come with my girlfriend and myself but I told him that **two's company and three's a crowd** so he stayed home.

  我朋友想和我及我的女朋友一起，但我告訴他多一個人就太擠了，所以他待在家裡。

T

測驗題 (Idiom Quizzes)

Choose an idiom to replace the expression in the blankets:

1. The company president was (dead and buried) before anyone knew he was dead.

   A at sixes and sevens   B on cloud nine   C six feet under   D all rolled up in one

2. After finding many problems with the engine design we decided to (go back and start over).

   A know a trick or two   B take five   C stand on our own feet   D go back to square one

3. I will return (very quickly).

   A in forty winks   B all in one piece   C one by one   D in two shakes of a lamb's tail

4. The girl is very selfish and is only concerned with (herself).

   A the three R's   B the lesser of the two   C number one   D her opposite number

5. I was (very happy) when I won a vacation trip during the winter.

   A on cloud nine   B a nine-day wonder   C dressed to the nines   D one for the books

測驗題 (Idiom Quizzes)

6. Our teacher makes sure that we have a good knowledge of (reading, writing, and arithmetic).

   A six of one and half of a dozen of the other　B the three R's　C number one
   D two of a kind

7. Solving a difficult problem by yourself is not easy and usually (it is better to work with another person to solve the problem).

   A there are no two ways about it　B two can play the game　C two wrongs don't make a right　D two heads are better than one

8. I tried to (add my comments) during the discussion between my father and my uncle.

   A put in my two cents worth　B cut both way　C give three cheers　D put two and two together

9. My friend has been (extremely successfully) with all of his business ventures.

   A batting a thousand　B six of one and half of a dozen of the other　C ten to one　D like two peas in a pod

10. The actress was (wearing her best dress) at the charity concert.

   A all rolled up in one　B a stitch in time　C at sixes and sevens　D dressed to the nines

測驗題 (Idiom Quizzes)

11. The schedule of my boss is always changing but (almost always) he is in his office on Monday morning.

    A at one time　　B nine out of ten　　C one by one　　D at the eleventh hour

12. We talked to the employees (individually) when we learned of the serious financial problems in the company.

    A on all fours　　B all in one　　C one by one　　D one and the same

13. Our supervisor is (a good member of the team) and he likes to spend time with the staff.

    A one of the boys　　B a quick one　　C a hundred to one shot　　D on cloud nine

14. The new sales manager is (attracting a lot of attention) and should rise quickly in our company.

    A our opposite number　　B a one-night stand　　C at one with everyone
    D a nine-day wonder

15. I stopped work for an hour in order to (have a short sleep).

    A look like a million dollars　　B get forty winks　　C cut both ways　　D have a stich in time

測驗題 (Idiom Quizzes)

Color Idioms

五顏六色

五顏六色 (Color Idioms)

A

◉ **as black as coal**：very black 像煤炭一樣黑

My friend's cat is **as black as coal**.
我朋友的貓像炭一樣黑。

◉ **as black as night**：very dark and black 黑暗

The old house was **as black as night** when we entered.
我們進入這棟舊房子時一片漆黑。

◉ **as black as pitch**：very black 像瀝青一樣黑

My face was **as black as pitch** after cleaning the stove all morning.
我的臉在清了一早上的爐子後像瀝青一樣黑。

◉ **as black as a skillet**：very black 像平底鍋底一樣黑

My hands were **as black as a skillet** when I finished working on the car engine.
在做完汽車引擎的工作後我的手像鍋底一樣黑。

◉ **as black as a stack of black cats**：very black 像一堆黑貓一樣黑

The little boy was **as black as a stack of black cats** after playing outside all day.
在外面玩了一天後這個小男孩像一堆黑貓一樣黑。

五顏六色 (Color Idioms)

- **as black as a sweep**：very dirty and black 像清掃煙囪的掃把一樣髒且黑

  My friend was **as black as a sweep** after he finished cleaning the basement.
  我朋友在清理完地下室後又髒又黑。

- **as black as the ace of spades**：very black 像撲克牌的黑桃一樣黑

  The horse in the parade was **as black as the ace of spades**.
  遊行中的那匹馬像黑桃A一樣黑。

- **as red as a cherry**：bright red 鮮紅

  The car was **as red as a cherry** after its new paint job.
  這車在新噴過漆後像櫻桃一般鮮紅。

- **as red as poppy**：bright red 鮮紅

  The mark on my arm was **as red as a poppy**.
  我手背上的記號像罌粟花一樣鮮紅。

- **as red as a rose**：intensely red 豔紅

  The morning sunrise was **as red as a rose**.
  早上的日出像玫瑰一樣豔紅。

- **as red as a ruby**：deep red 深紅

  The office assistant was wearing lipstick that was **as red as a ruby**.
  辦公室助理擦的口紅像紅寶石一樣深紅。

五顏六色 (Color Idioms)

- **as red as blood**：deep red 深紅

  The stain on the carpet was **as red as blood**.

  地毯上有一塊像血一樣紅的汙垢。

- **as white as a ghost**：very pale because of fear or shock or illness 因恐懼或震驚或生病而有的慘白

  My sister became **as white as a ghost** when she saw the man at the window.

  我姊姊在看到窗邊的人後臉色變得慘白。

- **as white as a sheet**：very pale 蒼白

  I felt terrible this morning and in the mirror I looked **as white as sheet**.

  今天早上我覺得很不舒服而且我看到鏡子裡的我一臉蒼白。

- **as white as the driven snow**：very white 雪白

  The fur on the dog was **as white as the driven snow**.

  這隻狗身上的毛像雪一樣白。

- **black and blue**：bruised 瘀血；烏青

  My shoulder was **black and blue** after I fell down the stairs.

  我摔下樓梯後肩膀上有瘀血。

五顏六色 (Color Idioms)

black and white：either good or bad, whether one way or the other way, oversimplified 黑白分明，不是這個就是那個；過於簡化

> Our boss sees everything in **black and white**.
> 我們老闆看事情不是黑就是白。

blackball (someone)：to exclude or ostracize someone socially, to reject someone 將某人排除 [排斥] 在社交圈外

> The businessman was **blackballed** in the industry because of his bad business practice.
> 這個生意人因惡劣的生意作法而被同業排斥。

black box：an electronic device such as a flight recorder that can be removed from an aircraft as a single package 黑盒子，飛機上用來記錄通話的電子裝置

> The investigators searched for a long time in order to find the **black box** of the airplane.
> 調查人員花了很長的時間搜尋飛機上的黑盒子。

black eye：a bruise near one's eye which makes it appear black 黑眼圈

> The man received a **black eye** when he bumped into the closed door.
> 這人因撞上緊閉的門而有黑眼圈。

blacklist (someone)：to exclude or ostracize someone, to write someone's name on a list if they break some rules 列入黑名單

> The sports federation **blacklisted** the swimmer because he was using steroids.
> 運動聯盟因這個游泳選手使用類固醇而將他列入黑名單。

五顏六色 (Color Idioms)

- **blackmail (someone)**：to extort or take money from someone by threatening him or her 勒索

  > The photographer tried to **blackmail** the famous actress with some photographs that he had taken.
  > 攝影師用他所拍的照片嘗試去勒索這名出名的女演員。

- **black market**：the place where goods or money are illegally bought or sold 黑市

  > We sold some cigarettes on the **black market** during our travels.
  > 我們在旅行期間在黑市上賣香菸。

- **black out**：to darken a room or building by turning off the lights 熄燈，燈火管制

  > During the war, people in the cities were forced to **black out** their windows so nobody could see them.
  > 戰爭期間，人們被迫將窗戶封上讓人看不到。

- **black out**：to lose consciousness 失去知覺

  > The man **blacked out** during the parade and he had to sit down and rest.
  > 這人在遊行中失去知覺而必須坐下休息。

- **blackout**：a temporary situation where you do not release some information 封鎖

  > The government decided to have a **blackout** regarding the political prisoner.
  > 政府決定封鎖這名政治犯的消息。

五顏六色 (Color Idioms)

- **black sheep (of a family)**：a person who is a disgrace to a family or group 害群之馬

  The man is the **black sheep** in his family and has not made a success of his life.

  這人是他家中的害群之馬而且一生也沒成功過。

- **black-tie event [affair]**：a formal event where guests wear semi-formal clothes with men wearing black bow ties with tuxedoes or dinner jackets 正式場合；男士必須穿著黑領結和小禮服的場合

  The award ceremony for the movie awards was a **black-tie event**.

  電影頒獎典禮是個正式場合。

- **blue blood**：someone from a noble or wealthy or aristocratic family 貴族或富有人家之後；富二代

  Many of the **blue bloods** of the town went to the opening of the opera.

  城裡很多的富二代都去參加歌劇首映。

- **blue in the face**：to be very angry or upset, to be excited and very emotional 臉變綠了

  I argued with my supervisor until I was **blue in the face**.

  我和我的主管爭執到臉都變綠了。

- **blue-ribbon**：of superior quality or distinction, the best of a group 藍帶；高品質好榮譽

  A **blue-ribbon** panel of experts were asked to suggest a new policy for the city.

  一群優秀的專家為城市新政策做建言。

五顏六色 (Color Idioms)

brown bag it：to take a lunch to work 帶便當上班

> I must **brown bag it** this week because the company cafeteria is closed.
>
> 因為公司餐廳關閉所以我這一週要帶便當。

carte blanche：the freedom or permission to do what you want 全權委任，自由處理

> The new manager was given **carte blanche** to change the policies in her department.
>
> 新經理在處理她部門政策作法上有完全自主的權限。

catch (someone) red-handed：to catch someone in the middle of doing something wrong 人贓俱獲

> The woman was **caught red-handed** when she tried to steal some cosmetics.
>
> 這女子在嘗試偷竊化妝品時被活逮。

chase rainbows：to try to get or achieve something that is difficult or impossible 追夢；通常指困難甚至於不可能的事

> My old school friend is always **chasing rainbows** and he never achieves anything.
>
> 我的學校老朋友總是在尋夢但從未達到目的。

dyed-in-the-wool：permanent, always (like wool that is dyed a certain color) 根生蒂固；像染過色的羊毛一樣變不了了

> My father is a **dyed-in-the-wool** conservative and he will probably never change.
>
> 我父親是個根生蒂固的保守派而他也不太可能改變。

五顏六色 (Color Idioms)

ears are red：one's ears are red form embarrassment 面紅耳赤

My **ears are red** after hearing what the teacher said about me.
在聽到老師說關於我的事後我變得面紅耳赤。

get gray hair：to have one's hair turn gray from stress 頭髮變灰白

Our teacher is **getting gray hair** from stress.
我們老師因壓力而頭髮變灰白。

get the blues：to become sad or depressed 變憂鬱

The dull cloudy weather has caused me to **get blues**.
陰沉多雲的天氣讓我變得憂鬱。

get the green light：to receive a signal to start or continue something 得到同意進行的信號

The city **gave us a green light** to begin the new project.
市政府同意我們開始新的計畫。

grass is always greener on the other side (of the fence)：a place or situation that is far away or different seems better than one's present situation 看不到或拿不到的都是好的

The man believes that the **grass is always greener on the other side** of the fence and he always wants to change jobs.
這個人總是覺得人家的更好所以老是換工作。

五顏六色 (Color Idioms)

◉ **the gray area**：something that is not clearly defined and does not conform to an existing set of rules, neither black or white, neither one way or the other 灰色地帶；模糊地帶

> The issue of the tax on children's toys is **a gray area** for the accountant.
>
> 兒童玩具的稅務問題對會計師而言是個模糊不清的地帶。

◉ **gray matter**：brains, intelligence 腦子；智慧

> I wish that my friend would use his **gray matter** more effectively when he is making his crazy plans.
>
> 我希望我的朋友在擬他那個瘋狂計畫時能多用腦子。

◉ **green**：to be inexperienced or immature 嫩；不成熟

> The young man is rather **green** and does not have enough experience to drive the large machinery.
>
> 這年輕人在駕駛大機具上仍顯經驗不足。

◉ **green around the gills**：look sick 病懨懨

> My friend looked **green around the gills** after the long bus ride.
>
> 我朋友在長途搭車後看起來病懨懨地。

◉ **green belt**：an area of field and trees around a town 環繞都市的綠地

> Our city has a policy to increase the **green belt** around the city.
>
> 我們城市有增加都市四周綠地的計畫。

green-eyed monster：jealousy 嫉妒

The woman was consumed by the **green-eyed monster** and it was affecting her life.

這女人因心中充滿妒忌而生活大受影響。

green thumb：a talent for gardening, the ability to make things grow 天生擅長園藝

My neighbor has a **green thumb** and she is able to grow one of the best gardens in our neighborhood

我的鄰居擅長園藝而且她的花園是附近最好的之一。

green with envy：to be very jealous, to be full of envy 妒忌

I was **green with envy** when I heard that my cousin would be going to the U.S. for a week.

當我聽到我堂 [表] 哥將要去美國一週時，我妒忌死了。

greenhorn：an untrained or inexperienced or naive person 生手

The young man is a **greenhorn** and he has much to learn about his new job.

這個年輕人是新手，他對於他的新工作還有很多要學的。

have a yellow streak：to become cowardly 變孬種

The man **has a yellow streak** and he will not defend you if you are having a problem.

這個人是孬種，當你有麻煩時他不會保護你。

五顏六色 (Color Idioms)

- **horse of a different color**：something totally separate and different 完全是另一回事

  I know that our boss would like to discuss that issue now but it is a **horse of a different color** and we should discuss it at another time.

  我知道老闆現在想要討論那事，但那事完全不如想像一般，我們該擇期再議。

- **in black and white**：in writing, officially 白紙黑字寫清楚；正式地

  I put down my complaint **in black and white**.

  我將我的埋怨寫下來。

- **in (someone's) black books**：to be in disgrace or in disfavor with someone 得罪某人

  The boy is **in** his girlfriend's **black books** because he was late for their date.

  這男孩因為約會遲到而得罪了他的女友。

- **in the black**：to be successful or profitable 有盈餘 [利潤]

  Our company has been **in the black** since they began to cut costs.

  我們公司在削減成本後就一直有盈餘。

- **in the pink (of condition)**：very healthy; very vigorous 精神飽滿，非常健康

  My grandmother was **in the pink** of condition when I saw her.

  當我看見祖母時她精神飽滿身體健康。

五顏六色 (Color Idioms)

- **in the red**：to be in debt, to be unprofitable 虧損

  The company has been **in the red** for three years now.
  這公司已經虧損三年了。

- **lend color to (something)**：to provide something extra to accompany something 增色

  The music in the play helped to **lend color to** the performance of the actors.
  劇中音樂為演員的表演增色不少。

- **like waving a red flag in front of a bull**：what you are doing will definitely make someone angry or upset 挑釁；自尋死路

  Talking about the city mayor with my father is **like waving a red flag in front of a bull**. He hates the city mayor.
  和我父親討論市長無異自尋死路。他恨市長。

- **local color**：the traditional features of a place which gives it its own character 當地特色

  The weekend vegetables market added much **local color** to the small town.
  週末蔬菜市場為小鎮增添些當地特色。

- **look at the world through a rose-colored glasses**：to see only the good things about something, to be too optimistic 過度樂觀

  My friend always **looks at the world through rose-colored glasses** and he does not believe that some people are dishonest.
  我的朋友太樂觀了，他不相信有人不誠實。

L

五顏六色 (Color Idioms)

off-color：in bad taste, rude 下流的

> The man told an **off-color** joke at the a party which made his wife angry.
> 這人在聚會中因說了個下流的笑話而讓他太太生氣。

off-color：not looking good/healthy; have no class or being vulgar 顏色不對

> We painted our kitchen in an **off-color** of white.
> 我們用怪怪的白色來漆我們的廚房。

once in a blue moon：very rarely 罕見

> We only go out for Japanese food **once in a blue moon** although we enjoy it very much.
> 儘管我們很喜歡但我們很少去餐廳吃日本菜。

out of the blue：without any warning, by surprise (like something that comes out of a blue sky) 晴天霹靂

> My friend decided **out of the blue** to quit his job and go to Europe.
> 我朋友突然決定辭掉工作去歐洲。

out of the red：out of debt 不再虧損

> Our company is finally **out of the red** and we are now making money.
> 我們公司總算不再虧損而賺錢了。

五顏六色 (Color Idioms)

- **painted the town red**：to go out and party and have a good time 尋歡作樂

  When my cousin came to visit us we decided to go out and **paint the town red**.
  當我表哥來拜訪我時，我們決定外出狂歡。

- **pink slip**：a termination notice from a job 解僱通知單

  I received my **pink slip** last week and I am now looking for a new job.
  我上個星期收到解僱通知，現在我正在找工作。

- **pitch-black**：very black, as black as pitch 一片漆黑

  The road was **pitch-black** and we could not see anything.
  路上一片漆黑我們什麼也看不到。

- **pot calling the kettle black**：the person who criticizes or accuses someone else is as guilty as the person he or she criticizes or accuses 五十步笑百步

  My friend criticized me for not changing jobs but that is like the **pot calling the kettle black**. She will not change jobs either.
  我朋友批評我不換工作，但那真是五十步笑百步。她自己也不換工作。

- **put (something) in black and white**：to write the details of a contract or something on paper 打合約

  I asked buyer to **put** the offer to buy my car **in black and white**.
  我要求買方把要買我車子的出價寫清楚。

P

五顏六色 (Color Idioms)

- **raise a white flag**：to indicate that you have been defeated and that you want to give up 投降

  > The soldiers **raised a white flag** and surrendered to the enemy.
  >
  > 士兵們向敵人投降。

- **red-carpet treatment**：to receive special or royal treatment 盛禮以待

  > I always receive **red-carpet treatment** when I go to visit my aunt.
  >
  > 我去拜訪嬸嬸時她總是盛禮以待。

- **red-eye**：an airplane flight that leaves late at night and arrives early in the morning 晚飛早到的飛機班次

  > We caught the **red-eye** flight last night and we are very tired today.
  >
  > 我們昨晚搭晚飛早到的班機所以今天很累。

- **a red flag**：a signal that something is not working properly or correctly 警告

  > The fallen trees along the road raised **a red flag** for the safety inspectors.
  >
  > 路邊的倒樹不啻是對安檢人員的警示。

- **red herring**：an unimportant matter that draws attention away from the main subject 分散注意力的東西

  > Talking about the other issue was a **red herring** that did not do anything to deal with today's problem.
  >
  > 討論其他事只不過是分散了對今天問題的注意力。

五顏六色 (Color Idioms)

- **red-hot**：very hot, creating much excitement or demand 火熱；搶手

  The new video game is **red-hot** and many people are waiting to buy one.

  新電玩非常搶手，很多人都等著買。

- **red in the face**：embarrassed 汗顏

  I became **red in the face** when the teacher asked me a question.

  老師問我問題時我感到難為情。

- **red-letter day**：a day that is memorable because of some important event 節日；紀念日

  It was a **red-letter day** when my sister received her graduation diploma.

  我姊姊收到文憑時是個特別的日子。

- **red tape**：excessive formalities if official business 繁文縟節

  Many businesses complain about the **red tape** that they must deal with in order to get anything done with the government.

  很多企業埋怨和政府打交道時必須處理很多繁文縟節。

- **roll out the red carpet**：to greet a person with great respect, to give a big welcome to someone 殷勤接待某人，以隆重方式歡迎

  The government **rolled out the red carpet** when the politician came to visit.

  政府在這位政治人物來訪時以隆重方式歡迎。

R

五顏六色 (Color Idioms)

sail under false colors：to pretend to be something that one is not 假冒

> The head of the company is **sailing under the false colors** and he does not really understand how the company works.
>
> 公司負責人是假冒的，他實際上並不知道公司是如何運作。

see pink elephant：to see things which are not really there because they are only in your imagination 看到幻覺

> The man was **seeing pink elephants** according to those who listened to his story.
>
> 根據聽到他說法的人說他看到了幻覺。

see red：to become very angry 盛怒

> My boss **saw red** when I told him that I would not be coming to work today.
>
> 當我告訴老闆說我今天不來上班時他發大脾氣。

see the color of (someone's) money：to prove that someone has enough money for something 見錢為憑

> The car dealer would not let me take the car until he **saw the color of** my **money**.
>
> 汽車經銷商不讓我拿車除非他看到我的錢。

show one's true colors：to show what one is really like or really thinking 真情，真正想的事

> I thought that the woman likes me but she **showed her true colors** when she began yelling at me on the phone.
>
> 我以為這女子喜歡我，直到她在電話上對我大叫才洩了底。

五顏六色 (Color Idioms)

- **talk a blue streak**：to talk very much and very rapidly 說話像機關槍一樣

  The woman beside me on the bus **talked a blue streak** for most of the journey.
  在公車上我旁邊的女子一路上滔滔不絕。

- **talk until one is blue in the face**：to talk until one is exhausted 說到聲嘶力竭

  I **talked until I was blue in the face** but I could not change my teacher's opinion about my essay.
  我向老師說得聲嘶力竭但依然無法改變他對我論文的看法。

- **tickled pink**：to be very pleased or delighted by someone or something 使某人非常愉快

  My mother was **tickled pink** that you visited her when you were in town.
  你進城時來拜訪我母親讓她很高興。

- **white elephant**：a useless possession (that often costs money to maintain) 大而無當的東西；蚊子館

  The new airport is a **white elephant** and nobody wants to use it.
  新機場因為沒人要使用而成了蚊子館。

- **white lie**：a harmless or small lie told to be polite or to avoid hurting someone's feeling 善意的謊言

  I told my girlfriend a **white lie** when I said that the dress matched her perfectly.
  當我告訴我女友洋裝很配她時，我說了一個善意的謊話。

T

五顏六色 (Color Idioms)

- **white sale**：the selling of towels or sheets at a reduced price 寢具組減價

  > We went to the **white sale** at the department to buy some new sheets.
  >
  > 我們在百貨公司寢具拍賣時去買了些床單。

- **whitewash (something)**：to cover up or gloss over faults or errors of wrongdoing 掩飾隱瞞，粉飾太平

  > The government was accused of trying to **whitewash** the scandal about the illegal money.
  >
  > 有人指控政府掩飾非法金錢上的醜聞。

- **with flying colors**：with great or total success 大獲全勝

  > My friend passed the course **with flying colors** and she now wants to celebrate.
  >
  > 我朋友在功課上得到優異的成績，現在她想慶祝。

- **yellow-bellied**：extremely timid, cowardly 膽怯的，孬種的

  > The man is **yellow-bellied** and is never willing to fight what is right.
  >
  > 這個人是個孬種而且絕不會為了對的事力爭。

W

測驗題 (Idiom Quizzes)

Choose an idiom to replace the expression in the blankets:

1. The girl was (very pleased) that she was chosen to represent her class at the competition.

   A blacked out   B tickled pink   C green with envy   D out of the blue

2. My boss is not very flexible and he always sees things (as either good or bad).

   A in the red   B off-color   C with flying colors   D in black and white

3. The government finally gave the city (permission) to build the new airport.

   A the green light   B a horse of a different color   C once in a blue moon
   D red tape

4. Our company has been (losing money) for three years now.

   A rolling out the red carpet   B yellow-bellied   C in the red   D green

5. It was a (memorable) day when the first person walked on the moon.

   A yellow-streak   B white-elephant   C red-herring   D red-letter

6. My brother passed the test to become a police officer (easily and with great success).

   A green   B with flying colors   C out of the blue   D tickled pink

測驗題 (Idiom Quizzes)

7. Our company told us (suddenly and without any warning) that our factory would close next month.

   A out of the blue　　B once in a blue moon　　C with flying colors　　D pitch-black

8. The mother (was very angry) when her daughter came home at three o'clock in the morning.

   A rolled out the red carpet　　B saw red　　C showed her true colors
   D looked at the world through rose-colored glasses

9. The man argued with his wife until he was (very angry) but still she would not agree with him.

   A brown bagging it　　B in the black　　C blue in the face　　D a pot calling the kettle black

10. I got to the swimming pool only (rarely) although I love to swim.

   A green around the gills　　B with flying colors　　C in the red　　D once in a blue moon

解答 (Answer Keys)

1.	B	2.	D	3.	A	4.	C	5.	D
6.	B	7.	A	8.	B	9.	C	10.	D

Food Idioms

民以食為天

民以食為天 (Food Idioms)

acquire a taste for (something)：to develop a liking for some kind of food or drink or something slse 養成對⋯的嗜好

> My friend has recently **acquired a taste for** classical music.
> 我朋友最近養成對古典音樂的嗜好。

apple of one's eye：someone or something that one likes a lot or likes more than others 極受珍愛的人事物；掌上明珠

> The little girl is the **apple of her grandfather's eye**.
> 這小女孩是她祖父的掌上明珠。

as busy as popcorn on a skillet：very active 非常忙碌（像平底鍋裡的爆米花）

> The children pretended to be **as busy as popcorn on a skillet** when the teacher entered the classromm.
> 當老師進入教室時，孩童們裝成很忙碌的樣子。

as cool as a cucumber：to be clam, to be not nervous or anxious 冷靜不緊張或不焦慮（cucumber：小黃瓜）

> The man is **as cool as a cucumber** and never worries about anything.
> 這人很冷靜而且從不會因任何事感到緊張。

as easy as apple pie [duck soup]：very easy 輕鬆容易

> The test that I wrote yesterday was **as easy as apple pie [duck soup]**.
> 昨天我寫的測驗很簡單。

162

民以食爲天 (Food Idioms)

as flat as a pancake：very flat 非常平；扁（pancake：鬆餅）

> The child's toy was **as flat as a pancake** after the car drove over it.
> 這個兒童玩具在被車子壓過後變扁了。

as hungry as a bear：very hungry 很餓

> I was **as hungry as bear** when I returned home from work yesterday.
> 我昨天下班回家時很餓。

as nutty as a fruitcake：silly, crazy 傻，瘋狂（fruitcake：水果蛋糕）

> The odd person in the supermarket was **as nutty as a fruitcake**.
> 在超級市場的怪男子有點瘋狂。

as red as a cherry：birhgt red 鮮紅

> My new sweater is **as red as cherry**.
> 我的新毛衣是鮮紅色的。

as slow as molasses in January：very slow 很慢（molasses：糖蜜）

> The little boy is **as slow as molasses in January** and he never gets his work finished on time.
> 這個小男孩動作很慢，他的工作永遠無法準時完成。

民以食為天 (Food Idioms)

as sour as vinegar：sour and disagreeable 讓人不舒服的酸（vinegar：醋）

The old man next door is **as sour as vinegar**.
隔壁的老先生尖酸的讓人受不了。

as sweet as honey [sugar]：very sweet 甜美

The librarian is **as sweet as honey** and everybody loves her.
這個圖書館管理員長得很甜美，每個人都喜歡她。

as thick as pea soup：very thick (can be used with fog as well as liquids) 濃；伸手不見五指

The fog was **as thick as pea soup** along the river bank.
河邊的濃霧讓人伸手不見五指。

as warm as toast：very warm and cozy 溫暖，溫馨

Our house was **as warm as toast** when we came in from the rain.
從雨中進入屋裡時我們感到一陣溫暖。

at one sitting：at one time, during the one period 一次，曾經一度

We ate most of the cake **at one sitting**.
我們一次就把蛋糕吃掉一大半。

back to the salt mines：to go back to (unpleasant) work 回去幹活

Lunch is over so let's go **back to the salt mines** for the afternoon.
午餐結束，讓我們繼續下午的工作。

民以食為天 (Food Idioms)

bad apple [egg]：a bad person 害群之馬

> The boy is a **bad apple** and he is always in some kind of trouble.
>
> 這男孩是個害群之馬，他總是會陷入某種麻煩中。

bear fruit：to yield or give results 有結果

> The woman's hard work at her business finally began to **bear fruit** when she started to make money.
>
> 這女子在她的事業上努力工作，在開始賺錢後總算有了結果。

best bib and tucker：one's best clothes 一個人最體面的衣著

> I wore my **best bib and tucker** for the wedding reception.
>
> 我穿上我最好的衣服出席婚禮。

big cheese：an important person, a leader 大 [重要] 人物

> The odd-looking man is a **big cheese** in his company so you should be nice to him.
>
> 那個長相奇怪的人是他公司裡的大人物，你得對他好些。

big enchilada：the biggest and most important thing or person 最重要的人 [事物]
（enchilada：辣椒肉餡玉米捲餅）

> The new manager is the **big enchilada** in our company.
>
> 我們公司的新經理是個大人物。

B

民以食為天 (Food Idioms)

binge and purge：to overeat and then to vomit 大吃大喝後強行催吐

> The young woman had eating problem; she would often **binge and purge** her food.
>
> 這女子有進食失調症；她常會大吃大喝後又去催吐。

bite off more than one can chew：to try to do or eat more than you can manage 做超出自己能力的事

> I **bit off more than I can chew** when I began to work two jobs.
>
> 我開始打兩份工時已超出我能負荷的量。

bite the hand that feeds one：to harm someone who does good things for you 不知感恩圖報

> I do not want to make my parents angry because I do not want to **bite the hand that feeds me**.
>
> 我不願意讓我父母親生氣，因為我不想不知感恩圖報。

bitter pill to swallow：something unpleasant that one must accept 難以接受的事物

> It was a **bitter pill to swallow** when I learned that I would not get the job.
>
> 當我知道工作無望時真是難以接受。

bolt down (something) /bolt (something) down：to eat something very quickly 匆匆吞下

> The man **bolted down** his food before going back to work.
>
> 這男子很快吞完他的食物後又繼續工作。

民以食為天 (Food Idioms)

- **born with a silver spoon in one's mouth**：to be born to a walthy family with many advantages 出生於富貴之家

  The boy was **born with a silver spoon in his mouth** and he never has to work very hard.

  這男孩出生於富貴之家，他從不需努力工作。

- **bottom up**：everybody should drink now (this expression is used at the end of a drink toast) 乾杯

  "**Bottom up**," our host said at the beginning of the dinner.

  我們的主人在晚宴開始時邀請大家乾杯。

- **bread and butter**：one's income or job that is used to buy the basic needs of life like food or shelter or clothing 基本日常的收入或生活需求

  Most people are worried about **bread-and-butter** issues like job and taxes.

  多數人擔心的平常事是工作和稅賦。

- **bread and water**：the most basic meal that is possible 基本食物

  Living on a tight budget, I can only have **bread and water** for meals.

  由於預算緊，我只能頓頓粗茶淡飯。

- **bring home the bacon**：to earn your family's living 養家活口

  Recently, I've been working hard to **bring home the bacon**.

  最近我努力工作來養家活口。

民以食為天 (Food Idioms)

○ **burn (something) to a crisp**：to burn something very badly 燒焦

> I **burned** the eggs **to a crisp** while I was talking on the phone.
>
> 我接電話時把蛋煎焦了。

○ **butter (someone) up/butter up (someone)**：to flatter someone in order to get his or her favor or friendship 阿諛奉承 [恭維] 他人，拍馬屁

> The man spends much time trying to **butter up** his boss so that he will not have to work so hard.
>
> 那男子試著拍老闆的馬屁，如此一來他就不必工作太辛苦了。

○ **buy a lemon**：to buy something that is worthless or does not work well 買了爛貨

> The used car that I bought is not very good; I think I **bought a lemon**.
>
> 我買的舊車不靈光；我想我買了個爛貨。

○ **can't stomach (something or someone)**：to dislike or hate someone or something 討厭甚至於憎恨某人或某事

> I **cannot stomach** the idea of meeting my old girlfriend.
>
> 我討厭要和舊女友見面的這件事。

○ **carrot and stick**：the reward for someone to do what you want or the punishment if they do not do what you want 賞罰兼施

> The government took a **carrot-and-stick** approach to remove the people who were protesting against the construction of the dam.
>
> 政府用賞罰兼施的作法來清除反對興建水壩的示威抗議者。

民以食為天 (Food Idioms)

cheese (someone) off/cheese off (someone)：to annoy or irritate or anger someone 激怒

I **cheesed off** my neighbor when I borrowed his ladder without telling him.
我在未告知就借用梯子時激怒了我的鄰居。

chew the fat (with someone)：to chat with someone 聊天

We stayed up late last night to **chew the fat** about our university days.
我們昨晚熬夜聊大學往事。

chips and dip：potato chips and something to dip them into before eating them 洋芋片和沾醬

We bought some **chips and dip** for the party.
我們為聚會買了些洋芋片和沾醬。

clear the table：to remove the dishes and other eating utensils from a table after eating 晚餐後清理乾淨桌子

We had to **clear the table** before we could eat our dessert.
我們在吃甜點前必須把桌子清理乾淨。

coffee break：a break from work to rest and drink coffe or tea 休息時間

We usually have a **coffee break** every morning at 10 o'clock.
我們通常每天早上十點時休息。

民以食為天 (Food Idioms)

- **come and get it**：come and eat 來吃吧

  > "**Come and get it!**" my mother called after she made dinner.
  > 母親在做完晚餐後叫：「來吃吧。」

- **compare apples and ornages**：to compare two things that are not similar and should not be compared 無從比較

  > It was like **comparing apples and oranges** when you compare your new girl-friend to old one.
  > 你無法比較你的新舊女友。

- **cook (someone's) goose**：to damage or ruin someone 阻攔他人成功

  > I think that I **cooked** my **goose** when I made a mistake at work today.
  > 我想我今天在工作上因犯錯而壞了自己的事。

- **cook (something) to perfection**：to cook something perfectly 煮東西煮到完美

  > The chef always **cooks** the food **to perfection** at his small restaurant.
  > 小餐廳主廚煮出來的東西總是完美無缺。

- **cook (something) up/cook up (something)**：to cook something; to make some kind of plan 煮東西；擬訂計畫

  > I plan to **cook up** some fish tonight.
  > 我今晚打算煮魚。
  >
  > I don't know what my girlfriend is **cooking up** for the weekend but we will probably do something interesting.
  > 我不知道我女友週末有什麼計畫，但我想我們可能會做些有趣的事吧。

C

民以食為天 (Food Idioms)

cook up a strom：to prepare a large quantity of food 準備大量的食物

My friend **cooked up a storm** for the party.

我朋友為了聚會而準備大量的食物。

couch potato：someone who spends a lot of time on a couch watching television 看電視殺時間的人

My cousin is a **couch potato** and he never wants to leave his house.

我表弟是個愛看電視殺時間的人，他從不想離開房子。

cream of the crop：the best of the group, the top choice 精華；菁英

Our company is always be able to hire the **cream of the crop** of university graduates.

我們公司總是能在大學畢業生中僱到菁英。

a cream puff：a person who is easily influenced or beaten 娘娘腔的柔弱男人

The boy is **a cream puff** and is always a victim of others' insults.

這男孩是娘娘腔，他總是他人侮辱的犧牲品。

cry over spilled [spilt] milk：to cry or complain about something that has already happened 覆水難收

You should not **cry over spilled milk**; the past is past and you cannot change it.

覆水難收；過去就過去，你也改變不了。

民以食為天 (Food Idioms)

(not one's) cup of tea：something that one does not enjoy or do well 不是某人感興趣的事物

Going to art galleries is **not my cup of tea** so I think I will stay home this evening.

去畫廊不是我感興趣的事，所以我想我今晚還是待在家裡。

cut the mustard：to succeed, to do adequately what needs to be done 出色達成任務，達到標準

The young man was not able to **cut the mustard** and he had to leave the company after only one year.

這年輕人在到職一年後因無法達到標準而離開公司。

dine [eat] out：to eat a meal at a restaurant 到餐廳用餐

I love to **dine out** at good restaurants.

我喜歡到好餐廳用餐。

done to a T [turn]：to be cooked just right 火候到家

The steaks were **done to a T** when my friend cooked them on the barbecue.

我朋友的火烤牛排真是火候到家。

down the hatch：swallow something (usually a drink) 一口吞 [嚥] 下

My drink was **down the hatch** before I could order another.

在我還沒再點一杯飲料前，我就把先一杯喝完了。

民以食爲天 (Food Idioms)

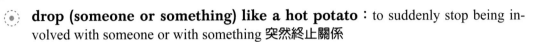

- **drop (someone or something) like a hot potato**：to suddenly stop being involved with someone or with something 突然終止關係

  The advertisers **dropped** the basketball star **like a hot potato** when he became involved in a scandal.

  廣告商在這個籃球明星涉及醜聞時就突然和他終止關係了。

- **duck soup**：a task that does not require much effort 輕而易舉的事；容易上當的人

  It was like **duck soup**. I easily finished my school project last night.

  我昨晚很容易地就把學校功課做完。小事一件。

- **eat and run**：to eat a meal and then quickly leave 吃完就走

  I had to **eat and run** in order to be on time for my evening class.

  我吃完就走免得晚上的課遲到。

- **eat crow**：being forced to something humiliating or disgusting 自食其果；被迫認錯

  I was forced to **eat crow** and apologized for the things I said about my co-worker.

  我被迫不情願地因所說的話向同事認錯並道歉。

- **eat dirt**：to act humble, to accept another person's insults or bad treatment 忍氣吞聲，低頭

  We made the boy **eat dirt** after he accused us of lying.

  那個男孩在指控我們騙人後，我們逼他低頭。

民以食為天 (Food Idioms)

eat high on [off] the hog：to eat expensive and high quality food 吃得好

> My friend has been **eating on the hog** since he got the new job.
> 我朋友在找到新工作後就吃香喝辣。

eat humble pie：to be humble, to admit one's error and apologize 低聲下氣地道歉

> Our boss was forced to **eat humble pie** after he made the wrong estimate for next year.
> 我們的老闆在錯估明年預算後被迫低聲下氣地道歉。

eat like a bird：to eat only a small amount of food 吃得很少

> The girl **eats like a bird** and is very slim.
> 這女子吃得很少而且很瘦。

eat like a horse：to eat a large about of food 吃得很多

> I usually **eat like a horse** after I work out.
> 在運動後我通常都吃得很多。

eat one's cake and have it too：to use or spend something and still keep it, to have something both ways 一箭雙鵰；腳踏兩條船

> The man refuses to give up anything and he always wants to **eat his cake and have it too**.
> 這男子拒絕放棄任何事物；他總是想腳踏兩條船。

民以食為天 (Food Idioms)

eat one's hat：to do something extraordinary or special if something that you do not think will happen actually happens 敢打賭；非常有把握

> I don't think my friend will arrive on time; if he does arrive here on time I will **eat my hat**.
>
> 我敢打賭我的朋友不會準時到這裡。

eat one's heart out：to be envious of someone or something 讓他人妒忌自己

> The winner of the award yelled, "**Eat your hearts out!**" to his rivals in the ceremony.
>
> 勝利者在頒獎典禮上大喊：「就是要你們難過！」

eat one's words：to take back something that one has said, to admit that something is not true 食言；把不實的話收回

> I told my boss that I would soon quit my job but later I had to **eat my words** and tell him that I want to stay.
>
> 我早先告訴老闆我要辭職，但後來卻不得不把話吃回去並告訴他我要留在公司。

eat out of (someone's) hands：to do what somelese wants 聽人差遣，供人使喚

> The young secretary is **eating out of** the manager's hands.
>
> 年輕的祕書受到經理的使喚。

eat (someone) for breakfast：to defeat someone easily 徹底擊敗某人

> The young wrestler was able to **eat** the older one **for breakfast**.
>
> 年輕的摔角選手徹底地擊敗了老選手。

民以食為天 (Food Idioms)

eat (someone) out of house and home：to eat a lot of food in someone's house 把人吃窮了

> The young athlete is **eating** his parents **out of house and home**.
>
> 這個年輕運動員把他爸媽吃窮了。

eat up (something)/eat (something) up：to eat everything on your plate；to enjoy or absorb or appreciate something 吃光；非常享受某事

> I **ate up** all my dinner and began my homework.
>
> 我把晚餐吃光後開始做功課。

egg (someone) on/egg on (someone)：to encourage someone to do something (often something wrong or bad or dangerous) 慫恿

> The boys **egged** their friends **on** to jump into the water.
>
> 男孩們慫恿他們的朋友跳入水中。

either feast or fmine：either too much or not enough of something 不是太多就是太少

> I usually have too much time or too little time. It's **either feast or famine**.
>
> 我要不就是時間太多要不就是時間太少。

everything from soup to nuts：almost everything that one can think of 一應俱全

> We bought **everything from soup to nuts** for our weekend holiday.
>
> 我們為週末假期買了所有的東西。

E

民以食爲天 (Food Idioms)

- **eyes are bigger than one's stomach**：the amount of food that one takes is greater than what one could possibly eat 拿的比能吃的多

  My **eyes were bigger than my stomach** and I took too much food at the buffet dinner.

  我在自助晚餐上拿的東西比能吃得還要多。

- **fat is in the fire**：a situation is bad or a person has serious problems 危機迫在眉睫；闖了大禍；大事不妙

  The **fat is in the fire** and the deadline is fast approaching for my final exams.

  大事不妙；期末考快到了。

- **feed one's face**：to eat 吃飯

  I stopped at a small restaurant after the game to **feed my face**.

  我在比賽後在一間小餐廳吃飯。

- **fine kettle of fish**：a mess, an unsatisfactory situation 困境；窘境

  It was a **fine kettle of fish** for me when I lost the keys to my apartment.

  我因遺失了公寓鑰匙而陷入困境。

- **food for thought**：something to think about, something that provides mental stimulation 值得深思的事

  The advice from the bank manager was **food for thought** when I made my financial plan.

  我在擬定財務計畫時，銀行經理的建議值得我深思。

F

民以食為天 (Food Idioms)

for peanuts：for very little money, for almost nothing 無價值之物，小數額

> I was able to buy a used computer **for peanuts**.
> 我花了很少的錢買了部舊電腦。

forbidden fruit：something that one finds attractive partly because it is illegal or immoral or prohibited 禁果

> Entering the old building was **forbidden fruit** for the young boys.
> 進入那棟老建築物對年輕的男孩而言是很誘惑但卻不能做的事。

fruits of one's labor：the results of one's work 工作的結果

> My father is retired now and is enjoying the **fruits of his labor**.
> 我父親現在退休了並且正在享受他努力工作的結果。

full of beans：feeling energetic, in high spirits 精神飽滿

> My friend is **full of beans** tonight and she does not want to stop talking.
> 我朋友今晚精神飽滿，她不想停止說話。

get oneself into a stew over (someone or something)：to be worried or upset about someone or something 擔心

> I try not to **get myself into a stew over** the rude remarks of my supervisor.
> 我試著不要因為我的主管的粗魯言論而擔心。

民以食為天 (Food Idioms)

go bananas：to become highly excited, to behave in a crazy way 失常，發瘋

The girl **went bananas** when her boyfriend forgot to buy her a birthday present.

這個女孩因男友忘了買生日禮物給她而發狂。

go beet-red：to become red in face because you are embrrrassed 因難為情而臉紅

I **went beet-red** when my friend told me the story.

我朋友告訴我的故事讓我面紅耳赤。

go on a binge：to eat or do too much of something 狂飲暴食

My friend **went on a binge** and ate too much chocolate.

我朋友吃了太多的巧克力。

good egg：a good person 好人

The man is a **good egg**. Everybody likes him a lot.

這人是個好人，所有人都很喜歡他。

(one's) goose is cooked：one has been discovered to have done something wrong and is now in trouble; one is finished; one's chances are ruined 東窗事發；機會毀了

I told a lie to my company. Now **my goose is cooked** and I am in much trouble.

我對公司撒了謊，現在東窗事發我麻煩大了。

民以食為天 (Food Idioms)

grab a bite to eat：to eat something usually quickly （匆匆忙忙）簡單地吃

> I will **grab a bite to eat** after the game today.
>
> 今天我在比賽後隨便吃點。

gravy train：a job or some work that pays more than it is worth 肥缺，好差事

> The job was a **gravy train** and I earned much money there.
>
> 這個工作是個肥缺，我在那裡賺了很多錢。

greatest thing since sliced bread：the greatest thing that there has ever been 最了不起的事或人

> My mother believes that the microwave oven is the **greatest thing since sliced bread**.
>
> 我母親深信微波爐是件最好的東西。

grist for the mill：something that can be used to bring advantage or profit 有利可圖的事

> The information that we got on the Internet was **grist for the mill** of our company's operations.
>
> 網路對我們公司運作而言是件有好處的事。

half a loaf is better than none：having part of something is better than having nothing at all 聊勝於無

> **Half a loaf is better than none** and I would rather work part-time than have no job at all.
>
> 聊勝於無；我情願兼差也不要沒有工作。

民以食為天 (Food Idioms)

- **half-baked**：to be not though about or studied carefully 淺薄的，沒頭腦的

  Our friend has a **half-baked** idea about starting a new business but most of us think that it will fail.

  我的朋友對生意有個不成熟的點子，但我們大部分的人都覺得它不會成功。

- **hand (something) to (someone) on a sliver platter**：to give a person something that has not been earned 雙手奉上

  The father **handed** everything **to** the boy **on a sliver platter** and now he is very spoiled and selfish.

  這父親什麼東西都給那男孩，現在那孩子被寵壞且自私。

- **hard nut to crack**：a difficult person or thing to deal with or get to know 棘手的事；難對付的人

  My friend is a very serious person and is a very **hard nut to crack**.

  我的朋友很嚴肅，他是個很難纏的人。

- **have a lot on one's plate**：to have many things to do or deal with, to be busy with many difficult activities 忙得不可開交

  I have a lot on my plate this week and I am busy.

  我這週有很多事，我會很忙。

民以食爲天 (Food Idioms)

have a pick-me-up：to have something that is refreshing or revig or ating 提神的東西；提神物

> Mary always carries a box of chocolate as **pick-me up**.
> 瑪莉總是帶盒巧克力當提神的東西。

have a sweet tooth：to have a desire to eat sweet foods 嗜甜食

> I **have a sweet tooth** and I love chocolate.
> 我喜歡甜食，我喜歡巧克力。

have a taste for (something)：to have a desire for a food or drink or something 對…有品味；喜歡

> The opera singer **has a taste for** fine jewery.
> 歌劇明星喜歡精緻的珠寶。

have a bigger fish to fry：to have more important things to do 還有更重要的事要做

> I **have a bigger fish to fry**; therefore, I don't want to waste time on trivials.
> 我還有更重要的事要做；因此，我不要把時間浪費在瑣事上。

have egg on one's face：to be embarrassed (because of obvious error) 因明顯錯誤而難為情

> The men **had egg on his face** now that he has admitted he was wrong about the whole incident.
> 這個人承認對這整件事有錯誤而感到難為情。

民以食為天 (Food Idioms)

- **have one's cake and eat it too**：to use or spend something and still keep it, to have something both ways 兩全其美

  I wanted to **have my cake and eat it too** when I wanted more holidays and more responsibility at work.

  我想要兩全其美，當我在工作時又要多休假又要多職責。

- **have one's finger in the pie**：to be involved in something 涉及

  The man **has his finegr in the pie** of many things at his workplace.

  這人在他工作場所涉及很多事情。

- **have one's finger in too many pies**：to be involved in too many things so that you cannot do any of them well 一心多用

  Our boss **has her finers in too many pies** and she cannot get anything done.

  我們老闆一心數用，她一件事也做不好

- **here's mud in your eye**：Drink up! (a drinking toast) 乾吧

  "Here's mud in your eye," I said as we drank a toast to my new job.

  我說：「乾吧！」我們為我的新工作乾杯。

- **hit the sauce**：to drink alcohol regularly 酗酒

  He began to **hit the sauce** after his wife died.

  他在他妻子死後開始酗酒。

民以食爲天 (Food Idioms)

hot potato：a question or argument that is controversial and difficult to settle 難以解決的問題或爭議

> This issue of building the nuclear plant is a **hot potato** for the town council.
> 興建核能電廠的這件事對市議會而言是燙手山芋。

icing on the cake：something that makes a good situation or activity even better 錦上添花

> I found a good job and the fact that I can work where I want is the **icing on the cake**.
> 我找到了個好工作，更好的事我還能在我想要的地方工作。

in a nutshell：briefly, in a few words 概括地說

> We went to the meeting and they told us **in a nutshell** about the plans for our company.
> 我們出席會議，他們概括地告訴我們公司的計畫。

in a pickle：in trouble, in a mess 陷入困境

> The boy was **in a pickle** when he lost the keys to the school cupboard.
> 男孩因丟掉了學校櫥櫃的鑰匙而陷入困境。

in a stew about [over] (someone or something)：to be worried or upset about someone or something 因事感到焦慮或不舒服

> My father is **in a stew over** the fact that the deadline for my college tuition is approaching.
> 我父親因我大學學費繳款日期逼近而感到焦慮。

民以食為天 (Food Idioms)

in one's salad days/in one's youth：a time when one is in experienced; lack of experience while in youth 年輕時

> My aunt was a beautiful woman in her salad days.
>
> 我阿姨 [嬸嬸] 在年輕時是個美人。

in the soup：in serious trouble, in a bad situation 左右為難

> The woman is **in the soup** now. She told her boss that she was sick but he saw her downtown shopping.
>
> 這女子出狀況了；她告訴老闆生病結果被他看到在市區逛街。

kill the fatted calf：to prepare an elaborate banquet in honor of someone 盛情款待，設宴歡迎

> We **killed the fatted calf** for my cousin after she returned from her trip abroad.
>
> 我們設宴歡迎剛從海外返國的表 [堂] 姊。

know which side one's bread is buttered：to know what is good or advantageous for you 知道自己利益所在

> My sister **knows which side** her bread is buttered when she visits our grandma.
>
> 我姊姊在探訪祖母時知道如何討好。

lay an egg：to give a bad performance of something 演出失敗

> The singer **laid an egg** during her concert last evening.
>
> 這位歌手在昨晚的演唱會中演出失敗。

民以食爲天 (Food Idioms)

- **life is a bowl of cherries**：only good things happen in life 生活中處處充滿歡喜

  Ever since my father retired from his job he believes that **life is a bowl of cherries**.

  自從我父親退休後他就相信生活中處處充滿歡樂。

- **like taking candy from a baby**：ver easy to do 輕而易舉

  I asked the department store to refund the money for my goods and they agreed. It was **like taking candy from a baby**.

  我輕而易舉地就讓百貨公司把我所買貨品的款項退給我。

- **like two peas in a pod**：very close or intimate with someone 長得很像；氣味相投

  The sisters are **like two peas in a pod** and they do everything together.

  這兩姊妹長得很像；她們所有事都一起做。

- **live off the fat of the land**：to grow one's own food, to live on the resources of the land 自力更生，自給自足

  The family **lives off the fat of the land** on their small farm.

  這家人在自己的小農場上自給自足。

- **make a meal of (something)**：to eat something, to eat one main dish or food as an entire meal 以…為主菜

  We **made a meal of** the fish that we caught in the lake.

  我們以在湖中捕到的魚為主菜。

民以食爲天 (Food Idioms)

- **make hamburger [mincemeat] out of (someone or something)**：to beat up or destroy someone or something 把某人打得一蹋糊塗

  > The big dog **made hamburger** out of the small dog.
  >
  > 大狗打敗小狗。

- **make one's mouth water**：to make someone hungry, to make someone want to eat or drink something 垂涎三尺

  > The restaurant is wonderful and when I see the menu it **makes my mouth water**.
  >
  > 這餐廳很棒，當我看到菜單時我就垂涎三尺了。

- **make (someone) eat crow**：to cause someone to admit an error or retract a statement 使某人認錯

  > The young man was **made to eat crow** when he made a rude comment.
  >
  > 年輕人因口出粗言而被要求收回。

- **meal ticket**：a thing or person that someone uses to get the money that need to live 飯票

  > The woman's nursing degree is her **meal ticket** to a flexible and good life.
  >
  > 這女子的護士學位是她過有彈性的好日子的飯票。

- **meat and potatoes**：basic simple and good food, simple tastes 最基本的，最重要的，最實際的

  > The man is a **meat-and-potatoes** person who enjoys the simple pleasure of life.
  >
  > 這男子是個務實的人，他享受單純的生活。

M

民以食爲天 (Food Idioms)

milk of human kindness：the natural kindness and sympathy that is shown to others 惻隱之心

> The woman at the community center is full of the milk of **human kindness**.
> 在社區中心的女子充滿了惻隱之心。

milk (something) for (someone)：to pressure someone into giving information or money 壓榨

> The man was trying to **milk** the elderly lady **for** money.
> 這男人向年老女子壓榨要錢。

neither fish nor bowl：not in any recognizable category 無法辨識

> I could not decide what the animal was. It was **neither fish nor bowl**.
> 我不知道這隻動物是什麼；我無法辨識。

not for all the tea in China：not for anything 不管怎樣也不…

> I will **not** lend my friend any more money **for all the tea in China**.
> 我無論如何都不再借錢給我朋友。

not know beans about (someone/something)：to know nothing about someone or something 什麼也不知道

> I don **not know beans about** repairing a car.
> 我對修車一無所知。

民以食爲天 (Food Idioms)

- **not worth a hill of beans**：worthless 沒價值

  > The man is a liar and what he says is **not worth a hill of beans**.
  > 這人是騙子，他所說的毫無價值。

- **on a diet**：to be trying to lose weight by eating less food 減肥

  > I have been **on a diet** for two months now.
  > 我現在已經減肥減了兩個月。

- **one man's meat is another man's poison**：something that one person likes may be disliked by someone else 青菜蘿蔔各有所愛

  > **One man's meat is another man's poison** and while my friend hates coffee, I love it.
  > 青菜蘿蔔各有所愛，我朋友恨咖啡而我卻愛死了。

- **out of the frying pan and into the fire**：to go from something bad to something worse 才離狼吻又入虎掌

  > The woman jumped **out of the frying pan and into the fire** when she realized that she was deeply in debt after quitting her job. Now her problems are much worse.
  > 這女子在辭職後才發現自己是負債累累；才離狼吻又入虎掌，她的問題越來越糟。

O

民以食為天 (Food Idioms)

out to lunch：to be crazy, to be uninformed 心不在焉的，愚蠢的，瘋癲癲的，不切實際的

> The woman is **out to lunch** and you should never believe what she tells you.
> 這女子有點瘋癲癲的，你不該相信她所說的事。

out for lunch：to be eating lunch away from one's work 外出吃午餐

> The bank manager was **out for lunch** when I went to meet him.
> 我去見銀行經理時，他外出吃午餐。

packed in like sardines：to be packed in very tightly 擠滿了

> The commuters were **packed in like sradines** in the subway car.
> 通勤者擠滿了地下鐵。

pick at (something)：to eat only little bits of something 把玩食物

> The boy is sick and will only **pick at** his food.
> 這個男孩生病了，他只在那玩他的食物。

pie in the sky：an idea or plan that you think will never happen 不可及的夢想，無法實現的諾言

> My cousin's plans of having his own business is nothing but a **pie in the sky**.
> 我表 [堂] 弟想要有自己生意的想法根本是不可實現的夢想。

P

民以食為天 (Food Idioms)

piece of cake：a task that is easily accomplished 輕而易舉地

> The job was a **piece of cake**. I finished it before the deadline.
> 這工作很容易，我早在期限前就完成了。

polish the apple：to flatter someone 奉承，拍馬屁

> Nobody likes the girl because she is always **polishing the apple** with her teacher.
> 因這女孩總是拍老師的馬屁所以沒人喜歡她。

put all one's egges in one basket：to risk everything at once 風險集中

> I don't want to **put all my eggs in one basket** and only invest money in real estate.
> 我不要集中風險把錢全投資在房地產上。

put on the feed bag：to eat meal (like a horse would) 吃飯

> We **put on the feed bag** right after we got home.
> 我們一回家就吃飯。

put on weight/put weight on：to gain weight 變胖

> Athlets sometimes need to **put on weight** to compete.
> 運動員有時須變胖才能競爭。

P

民以食爲天 (Food Idioms)

◉ **rotten apple**：a bad person 爛蘋果；不好的人或事

> Sometimes there is one person who is a **rotten apple** in a group of people.
> 有時，一顆老鼠屎壞了一鍋粥。

◉ **rotten to the core**：to be completely worthless (like a rotten apple) 壞到骨子裡

> The political system is **rotten to the core** and everybody knows that it must be changed.
> 政治制度壞透了，大家都知道它需要被改變。

◉ **rub salt in (someone's) wound**：to try to make someon'es unhappiness or misfortune worse 加深創傷

> I did not mention the car accident to my friend for I did not want to **rub salt in** his **wound**.
> 我沒提車禍的事，因為我不想讓我朋友痛上加痛。

◉ **salt of the earth**：good [basic, honest, ordinar] people 社會中堅

> Our new neighbors are the **salt of the earth**; they come from all walks of life.
> 我們的鄰居是社會中堅；他們來自各行各業。

◉ **salt (something) away/sale away (something)**：to save or gather money or some other item 儲存

> I am **salting away** much money from my work.
> 我在工作上存了許多錢。

R

民以食為天 (Food Idioms)

- **save (someone's) bacon**：to help someone from failing or having trouble 救援；協助

  My friend **saved** my **bacon** when he helped me with the job that I could not do.

  我朋友在我無法做的工作上幫了我。

- **sell like hotcakes**：to sell quickly or easily 賣得容易賣得好

  The new CD by Lady GaGa is **selling like hotcakes**.

  女神卡卡的新唱片賣得又快又好。

- **sink one's teeth into (something)**：to take a bite of some kind of food, to get really involved in something 卯足了勁

  I am trying hard to **sink my teeth into** the project at work.

  我卯足勁投入手中的計畫。

- **slice of the cake [pie]**：a share of something (monet, etc.) 分一杯羹

  The government wants a **slice of the cake** from the new casinos.

  政府要在新賭場的事上分一杯羹。

- **small potatoes**：something that is not very big or important compared with other things or people 小角色，不重要的事

  The amount of money for the stadium is **small potatoes** compared to the total cost of the Olympics.

  體育館的錢和奧運會的費用相比實在是微不足道。

S

民以食為天 (Food Idioms)

- **so clean you can eat off the floor**：very clean 非常乾淨

  > My mother's kitchen is **so clean that you can off the floor**.
  > 我母親的廚房非常乾淨。

- **soup up (something)/soup (something) up**：to make something faster or more powerful by changing or adding something 增強車的馬力

  > My neighbor decided to **soup up** his car.
  > 我鄰居決定增加他的車子的馬力。

- **spill the beans**：to tell a secret to someone who is not supposed to know about it 洩密

  > Please do not **spill the beans** about my plans to return to school next year.
  > 請別把我明年回學校的事洩露出去。

- **spoon-feed (someone)**：to help someone too much when you are trying to teach him or her something 填鴨式教育；溺愛

  > We had to **spoon-feed** the new employees who we were teaching about the new computer system.
  > 我們在教新進員工新電腦系統時必須用填鴨的方式。

- **square meal**：a good filling meal 紮實的一頓

  > I was very busy at work last week and I did not have time for a **square meal** until Sunday.
  > 我上週很忙直到星期天才吃頓像樣的飯。

民以食為天 (Food Idioms)

- **stew in one's juice**：to suffer from something that you yourself have cause to happen 自作自受，自吹自擂，作繭自縛

  The man caused the problem himself and he is not having **stew in his juice**.

  這人是自作自受。

- **stick to one's ribs**：to last a long time and to fill one up 飽實

  The meal that my grandmother made **stuck to my ribs**.

  祖母做的飯讓我有飽足感。

- **take (something) with a grain of salt**：not to take something that someone has said seriously 半信半疑

  You should **take** everything that the supervisor says **with a grain of salt** because he likes to exaggerate things.

  你在聽主管所說的事情時要有所保留，因為他喜歡誇大其詞。

- **take the cake**：to be the best or worst of something 最棒的；壞到極點的

  The behavior of the young girl **takes the cake**; it's terrible.

  這年輕女子的行為壞透了。真可怕。

- **teach one's grandmother to suck eggs**：to try to sell someone who has more knowledge than you know how to do something 班門弄斧

  I tried to teach my friend about computers but he is a computer expert. It was like **teaching my grandmother to suck eggs**.

  我教朋友電腦但他是個電腦專家；我在班門弄斧。

T

民以食為天 (Food Idioms)

⊙ **teething problems**：difficulties or problems that happen in the early stages of a project or activity 創業階段的困難

> The new project which we were trying to start had many **teething problems**.
>
> 我們想要開始的事業有許多創業時的困難。

⊙ **that's the way the cookie crumbles**：that's life, those things happen 人生就是這麼回事

> **That's the way cookie crumbles**, I thought when I learned that I would not get the new job.
>
> 我在知道新工作無望時告訴自己人生就是這麼回事。

⊙ **there is no such thing as a free lunch**：you can't get something without working for it or pay for it 天下沒有不勞而獲的事

> **There is no such thing as a free lunch** and you must work hard if you want to get something in life.
>
> 天下沒有不勞而獲的事，如果在生命中想要某件事就要努力。

⊙ **too many cooks spoil the broth [stew]**：too many people trying to do something will cause problems 人多手雜

> **Too many cooks spoil the broth** and having too many people on the project was making it difficult to do anything.
>
> 人多手雜；一個計畫中太多人只會製造問題。

T

民以食爲天 (Food Idioms)

- **top banana**：the person who is the boss or the top person in a group or organziation
老闆

> The famous actor in the movie was the **top banana** in the story.
> 這位名演員在電影中扮演老闆的角色。

- **tub of lard**：a fat person 胖子

> The young boys always call the fat boy a **tub of lard**.
> 那些年輕男孩們總是叫那個胖男孩胖子。

- **tuck into (something)**：to eat something with energy and enjoyment 大吃特吃

> We **tucked into** our dinner when we sat down at the table.
> 我們坐下後盡情享受晚餐。

- **turn beet-red**：to become red in the face because you are embarassed 面紅耳赤

> The girl **turned beet-red** when her friend asked about her boyfriend.
> 當這個女孩的朋友問她有關她男朋友的事時她就變得面紅耳赤。

- **upset the applecart**：to ruin a plan or event by a surprise or accident 破壞某人的
計畫或好事

> Everything was going well at the picnic until my former boyfriend arrived and
> **upset the applecart**.
> 野餐一切進行順利直到我前男友出現壞了好事。

T

民以食爲天 (Food Idioms)

variety is the spice of life：differences and changes make life interesting 變化讓生活充滿情趣

> **Variety is the spice of life** and I enjoy doing many different things.
>
> 變化讓生活充滿情趣，我喜歡做不同的事。

walk on eggshells [eggs]：to be very cautious and careful about someone so that he or she does not become angry 戰戰兢兢，小心翼翼

> I must **walk on eggeshells** when I ask my boss a question.
>
> 我問老闆問題時一定要小心翼翼的。

what's good for the goose is good for the gander：what is good for one person should be good for another person as well 對母鵝好的事也能適用在公鵝身上；一體適用

> **What's good for the goose is good for the gander** and you should not ask your child to so something if you will not do it yourself.
>
> 一體適用；你不該要求小孩做你自己不願做的事。

whet (someone's) appetite：to cause someone to be interested in something and want to learn more about it 引起他人好奇；吊胃口

> The introduction to playing a musical instrument helped to **whet** my **appetite** to learn about music.
>
> 演奏樂器的介紹引起我想要知道更多和音樂相關事情的好奇。

民以食為天 (Food Idioms)

whole ehchilada：everything, all of something 所有的

> I decided to buy the **whole enchilada** when I saw the set of dishes and kitchen goods.
>
> 當我看到整組餐盤和廚房產品時讓我有了買全套的決定。

wine and dine (someone)：to treat someone to an expensive meal, to entertain someone in a lavish manner 以盛宴款待他人

> My uncle often has to **wine and dine** his important business clients.
>
> 我叔叔常常需要以盛宴款待他重要的客戶。

worth one's salt：to be a good worker, to be worth what one is paid 物超所值

> The man has only been working here for a month but quickly he is proving that he **worth his salt**.
>
> 這人只在這裡工作一個月但已經證明他是物超所值。

you can't make an omelette without breaking the eggs：you cannot do something without causing some problems or having some effects 吃燒餅沒有不掉芝麻的

> **You can't make omelette without breaking the eggs** and if you want to change the work schedules, then you are going to cause problems.
>
> 吃燒餅沒有不掉芝麻的；你要改變工作時間，那麼你就會造成問題。

測驗題 (Idiom Quizzes)

Choose an idiom to replace the expression in the blankets:

1. The teacher said that the boy was (her favorite).

   A polishing the apple   B a piece of cake   C out to lunch   D the apple of her eye

2. The woman was (very calm) during the job interview.

   A as cool as a cucumber   B in the soup   C full of beans   D the cream of the crop

3. It is not (something that appeals to me) but I will go to the art gallery with you if you want.

   A my bread and butter   B my duck soup   C my cup of tea   D my gravy train

4. Our boss told everyone that they could have a holiday next week but he later had to (retract what he had said) and cancel it.

   A make his mouth water   B eat his words   C polish the apple   D take it with a grain of salt

5. I explained (briefly) what my friend needed to know but he still was not satisfied.

   A in a nutshell   B out of the frying pan and into the fire   C in the soup
   D as cool as a cucumber

測驗題 (Idiom Quizzes)

6. I worked all summer and was able to (save) a lot of money to go back to school.

   A butter up   B egg on   C take with a grain of salt   D salt away

7. The woman is a very good worker and is definitely (being paid what she deserves).

   A worth her salt   B souped up   C nutty as fruiscake   D a hot potato

8. Please do not (tell anyone) about my plans to get married next year.

   A hit the sauce   B get egg on your face   C spill the beans   D eat humble
   pie

9. The clerk is always trying to (flatter) his boss in order to get a raise.

   A big cheese   B butter up   C bread and butter   D egg on

10. The toys have been (selling very rapidly) since they were released last month.

   A upsetting the applecart   B selling like hotcakes   C worth their salt
   D half-baked

11. I stopped to (chat) with an old friend on my way to work this morning.

   A chew the fat   B eat my words   C cut the mustard   D cry over spilt milk

測驗題 (Idiom Quizzes)

12. My friend was told that he was not able to (succeed) and could not join the football team again this year.

   A bring home the bacon   B eat crow   C stew in his own juice   D cut the mustard

13. Our neighbor has a lot of stress and recently she had begun to (drink heavily).

   A eat her words   B have egg on her face   C hit the sauce   D upset the applecart

14. The man went (from something bad to something worse) when he got angry and quit his job.

   A out of the frying pan and into the fire   B as cool as a cucumber   C to cry over spilt milk   D for peanuts

15. Passing the exam was (very easy) because I spent a lot of time studying last week.

   A the cream of the crop   B out to lunch   C in the soup   D a piece of cake

測驗題 (Idiom Quizzes)

解答 (Answer Keys)

1. D	2. A	3. C	4. B	5. A
6. D	7. A	8. C	9. B	10. B
11. A	12. B	13. C	14. A	15. D

Clothes Idioms
佛要金裝人要衣裝

air one's dirty linen in public：to discuss one's private quarrels or problems in front of others 家醜外揚

The man does not like his wife to **air his dirty linen in public** when they are with friends.

這男子不喜歡他太太在朋友面前說糗事。

all drssed up：dressed in one's best clothes 盛裝

The girls were **all dressed up** for the evening.

女孩們為了晚上全都穿上最好的衣服。

as comfortable as an old shoe：very comfortable, very familiar 如舊鞋般地舒適；熟悉地

I felt **as comfortable as an old shoe** when I entered my aunt's house.

我到叔 [舅] 母家時感到非常適應熟悉。

as common as an old shoe：low class, gadly mannered 粗俗低級

The young woman is **as common as an old shoe**.

這女子非常粗鄙。

as tough as an old boot：vert tough, not easily moved by feelings such as pity 冷酷無情

The old lady is **as tough as an old boot** and never shows her feeling at all.

這個老女人很冷酷，她從不將感受表現出來。

佛要金裝人要衣裝 (Clothes Idioms)

B

- **at the drop of a hat**：without waiting or planning, immediately, promptly 立刻；欣然地

  > Our boss will stop working and help someone **at the drop of a hat** when needed.
  >
  > 有需要時，我們的老闆會立即去幫助人。

- **beat the pants off (someone)**：to beat someone severely, to win against easily in a race or a game 打垮某人

  > Our team **beat the pants off** the other team very easily.
  >
  > 本隊輕鬆地擊敗另外一隊。

- **best bib and tucker**：one's best clothing 最漂亮的衣物

  > The man wore his **best bib and tucker** to the meeting.
  >
  > 這男子穿上他最好的衣服出席會議。

- **bet one's boot**：to bet everything that one has 賭上一切

  > I will **bet my boots** that my friend will not have enough money to go on a holiday.
  >
  > 我願對我朋友沒錢度假一事賭上一切。

- **birthday suit**：complete nakedness 全裸

  > The little boy was running through the park in his **birthday suit**.
  >
  > 這小男孩全身赤裸地跑過公園。

佛要金裝人要衣裝 (Clothes Idioms)

bore the pants off (someone)：to fighetn someone very badly 令人恐懼或厭煩

> The new teacher **bored the pants off** the students.
>
> 新老師嚇到所有學生了。

buckle down to (do something)/buckle down and (do something)：to make a big effort to so something, to give one's complete attention or effort to do something 努力從事，傾力去做

> The teacher told the girl that she must **buckle down and** begin to work harder than before.
>
> 老師告訴女孩要比以前還盡力地去努力。

burn a hole in one's pocket：to stimulate someone to spend money quickly 有錢必花光

> My money is **burning a hole in my pocket** and I will probably spend it quickly.
>
> 我想我很快就會把錢花光。

burst at the seams：to be too full or too crowded 擁擠

> The train was **bursting at the seams** as everyone waited to go on their holidays.
>
> 因為大家都去度假所以火車上擠滿了人。

by the seat of one's pants：by luck and with very little skill 幸運

> I was able to complete the course **by the seat of my pants**.
>
> 我很幸運地完成了這門課。

佛要金裝人要衣裝 (Clothes Idioms)

cap and gown：the academic cap and gown that is worn during graduation ceremonies 畢業服

> Everybody was wearing their **cap and gown** for the university graduation ceremony.
>
> 所有人都在大學畢業典禮上穿著畢業服。

catch (someone) with their pants down：to surprise someone in an embarrassing situation or doing something that they should not be doing 逮個正著

> The sales manager was **caught with his pants down** when he was asked for the sales figures that he did not have.
>
> 業務經理因為沒有該有的銷售數字而被逮個正著。

charm the pants off (someone)：to use very nice or charming behavior to persuade someone to do something 迷死人；巴結

> I was able to **charm the pants off** the man in the job interview and I got the job.
>
> 我因在面談時迷死主考官而得到工作。

cloak-and-dagger：involving secrecy and plotting 與祕密或陰謀有關的

> The spy was involved in some **cloak-and-dagger** operations.
>
> 這個間諜涉及一些祕密活動。

coat and tie：a jacket or a sports coat and a necktie 西裝領帶

> The company asked everyone to wear a **coat and tie** to the company dinner.
>
> 公司要求所有人穿西裝打領帶出席公司晚餐。

佛要金裝人要衣裝 (Clothes Idioms)

come apart at the seams：to be in a bad situation and to begin to lose control, to become extremely upset 完蛋失敗；關係破裂

Our team is **coming apart at the seams** since our coach left.
教練離開後我們的隊伍四分五裂。

The man is **coming apart at the seams** since he lost his job.
這人自失掉工作後就完蛋了。

come into fashion：to become fashionable 流行

Recently, the mini-skirt has **come into fashion** again.
最近迷你裙又流行了。

cut a fine figure：to look good, to dress well 儀表甚佳；展露頭角

The man **cut a fine figure** when he entered the dining room.
這人打扮入時地進入餐廳。

cut from the same cloth：to share a lot of similarities 非常相似

The two boys are **cut from the same cloth** and are similar in every way.
這兩個男孩在所有事情上都很相像。

decked out in (something)：to be dressed in fancy clothes 穿上最好的衣服

The actress was **decked out in** a beautiful dress at the ceremony.
女明星在典禮上穿著漂亮的衣裳。

佛要金裝人要衣裝 (Clothes Idioms)

- **die with one's boots on**：to die while still active in one's work or while doing a job 死在工作崗位上

  The man worked hard all his life and **died with his boots on** when he had a heart attack at the factory.

  這人終生努力工作且最後在工廠心臟病發作而死去。

- **(do something) like it is going out of fashion [style]**：to use [buy, eat] much or too much of something 唯恐不及

  My friend is spending money **like it is going out of fashion**.

  我朋友花錢就像唯恐來不及一樣。

- **don sackcloth and ashes**：to behave in a way thet shows that you are very sorry for something that you have done wrong 低調道歉

  The man was asked to **don sackcloth and ashes** to repent for his terrible mistake.

  這人被要求對所犯錯誤低調道歉。

- **down-at-the heels**：to be shabby, to be poorly dressed 衣衫襤褸

  The man looked **down-at-the-heels** after he was fired from his job.

  這人在從工作被開除後穿著就非常破舊。

- **dressed to kill**：wearing one's finest clothes 精心打扮

  The woman was **dressed to kill** when I saw her at the meeting.

  這女子在出席會議時精心打扮。

佛要金裝人要衣裝 (Clothes Idioms)

dressed to the nines [teeth]：to be dressed elegantly, to be dressed very well 盛裝打扮

> The couple were **dressed to the nines** when they went to the opening of the new theater production.
>
> 這對夫婦盛裝出席新劇作的首演。

dress up：to wear one's best clothes 盛裝

> I decided to **dress up** for dinner on Saturday night.
>
> 我決定盛裝出席週六的晚宴。

emperor's new clothes：used when many people believe something that is not true, a situation in which people are afraid to criticize something because everyone else seems to think that it is good or important 礙於眾意而不揭穿

> It was like the **emperor's new clothes** when nobody would criticize the popular politician although he was doing many bad things.
>
> 沒有人願意去批評受歡迎卻作惡多端的政治人物，這就像國王的新衣一般。

fall apart at the seams：to separate at the seams, to fall apart 開線

> My backpack was **falling apart at the seams** so I bought a new one.
>
> 我的背包開線了，所以我買了一個新的。

佛要金裝人要衣裝 (Clothes Idioms)

- **feather in one's cap**：something to be proud, an honor 值得驕傲的事物，榮譽

  Winning the speech contest was a **feather in the boy's cap** and a great honor.
  贏得演講比賽對這個男孩而言是值得驕傲的事。

- **fill (someone's) shoes**：to take the place of another and do as well as he or she would do 取代某人的工作或地位

  It will be difficult for the woman to **fill the shoes** of the previous supervisor.
  這女子想要取代前任主管的工作是相當困難的。

- **fine-tooth [toothed] comb**：great care, careful attention so as not to miss anything 龜毛挑剔

  We went over the room with a **fine-tooth comb** but we were unable to find the lost credit card.
  我們很仔細地搜尋房間但未能找到遺失的信用卡。

- **fit like a glove**：to fit perfectly 合適，合身

  The woman's new dress **fits like a glove** so she was very happy.
  這個女人的新衣服非常合身，所以她非常高興。

- **fly by the seat of one's pants**：to do something by instinct rather than by knowledge or logic 在沒有客觀標準下摸索行事

  I was forced to **fly by the seat of my pants** when my computer broke and I had to try to fix it.
  電腦壞時我被迫要自行摸索去修好它。

佛要金裝人要衣裝 (Clothes Idioms)

- **get all dolled up**：to get dressed up in one's best clothes 裝扮起來

  The woman **got all dolled up** for the party.

  這女子為了聚會而裝扮起來。

- **get along on a shoestring**：to manage with very little money 勉強過日子

  I had to **get along on a shoestring during** university.

  我在大學時必須勉強過日子。

- **get the boot**：to be fired from a job, to be told to leave a place 開除；趕走

  I **got the boot** from my first job in high school.

  我第一次被開除是在高中。

  The man **got the boot** from the restaurant for smoking.

  這人因為抽菸而被從餐廳中趕走。

- **give (someone) the boot**：to fire someone from a job, to force someone to leave a place. 開除 [趕走] 他人

  The manager **gave** the man **the boot** when he began yelling in the restaurant.

  這人因為在餐廳中叫囂而被經理趕走。

- **go out of fashipon [syle]**：to become unfashionable 落伍，過時

  Strpied pants have recently **gone out of fashion**.

  條紋褲最近過時了。

佛要金裝人要衣裝 (Clothes Idioms)

- **give (someone) the shirt off one's back**：to be very generous to someone 對他人慷慨大方

  My uncle is very kind ans he will **give the shirt off his back**.
  我叔叔很仁慈且大方。

- **hand in glove with (someone)**：very close with someone 關係密切

  The supervisor and manager work **hand in glove** to create a positive atmosphere in the company.
  主管和經理一起努力為公司營造出一種正面的氣氛。

- **handle [treat] (someone) with a kid gloves**：to handle someone very gently and carefully because you do not want to upset him or her 小心翼翼地處理

  You must **handle** the new employee **with kid gloves** because he is very sensitive.
  新員工很敏感，你一定要小心對待。

- **a hand-me-down**：a piece of clothing that is given to someone after another person does not need it 別人用過的舊東西

  My father wore many **hand-me-down** clothes when he was a child.
  我父親在小時候穿了很多人家不要的舊衣服。

- **hang on (someone's) coattails**：to have one's fortune or success depend on another person 依賴他人致富成功

  The man is **hanging on the coattails** of his father.
  這人依賴他父親致富。

佛要金裝人要衣裝 (Clothes Idioms)

hang one's hat (somewhere)：to live or take up residence somewhere 住所

I want to move and **hang my hat** in a small town somewhere.

我想要搬到一個小城市居住。

hang up one's hat：to leave a job (usually after a long career) 去職，離開工作

The man decided to **hang up his hat** after forty at his job.

在工作四十年後，這人決定退休了。

have a bee in one's bonnet：to have a fixed idea that stays in one's mind 偏執的念頭，揮之不去的念頭

The man **has a bee in her bonnet** about starting a new business.

這女子一直把開始自己新事業的念頭放在心上。

have a card up ones' sleeve：to have a reserve plan or a secret advantage 留一手，錦囊妙計

I don't know the manager's plans but I think that he **has a card up in his sleeve** and he will soon make important announcement.

我不知道經理有何計畫，但我認為他留了一手而且他很快就要宣布了。

have an ace up one's sleeve：to have something that you can use to gain advantage 袖裡乾坤，王牌

The football players were ready to go on strike but the team owners **had an ace up their sleeve** and offered more money and stopped the strike.

足球員準備罷工但球隊老闆有王牌，他用多給錢化解了罷工。

佛要金裝人要衣裝 (Clothes Idioms)

have ants in one's pants：to be restless, to be nervous 緊張，坐不住

> The teacher told the little boy that he was moving around like he **had anits in his pants**.
>
> 老師告訴小孩說他動來動去就好像褲子裡有螞蟻一樣。

have (someone) in one's pocket：to have control over someone 完全控制一個人

> The large union **has** the city mayor **in their pocket**.
>
> 工會完全控制住市長。

hit (someone) below the belt：to do something in an unfair or cowardly way 勝之不武，出陰招

> Mr friend was **hitting below the belt** when he criticized me after I told him my true feeling.
>
> 在我告訴他我真正的感覺後，我的朋友竟批評我，真是低級！

hot under the collar：to be very angry 盛怒

> Our boss is **hot under the collar** today because three of the staff came late.
>
> 我們老闆今天因有三名員工來晚了而大發雷霆。

if the shoe fits wear it：if what is being said in general describes you then it probably means you 若有人影射的是你，那可能就是你；對號入座

> You should not criticize others for something that you should do yourself. Remember, **if the shoe fits wear it**.
>
> 別因自己不做而去批評他人；記住，該你做就要由你做。

佛要金裝人要衣裝 (Clothes Idioms)

in fashion：fashionable 流行

> Very thin necktie is not **in fashion** now.
> 窄領帶現在不流行。

in one's Sunday best：in one's best clothes that you would wear to go to worship in a church 最好的衣服

> I was dressed **in my Sunday best** when I went for the job interview.
> 我在面試時穿上了我最好的衣服。

in (someone's) shoe：in another person's place or position 將心比心，易地而處

> I would hate to be **in cousin's shoe** now that he has lost his job.
> 我表弟失掉了工作，我現在可不希望和他易地而處。

keep one's shirt on：to keep from losing one's temper or from getting excited, to be calm or patient 沉住氣

> **Keep your shirt on**. You shouldn't get so excited about such a small problem.
> 沉住氣。你不該為這種小問題而激動。

keep (something) under one's hat：to keep something secret 祕密

> I plan to **keep** my plans to look for a new job **under my hat**.
> 我計畫把找個新工作的事當成祕密。

佛要金裝人要衣裝 (Clothes Idioms)

- **laugh up one's sleeve**：to laugh quietly to oneself 偷笑

  I was **laughing up my sleeve** when I learned that my friend would have to clean the bathroom at work.

  我聽到我朋友在上班的地方要打掃廁所時不禁偷笑。

- **lick (someone's) boots**：to believe in a servile manner toward someone 拍馬屁，低聲下氣

  Our boss wants everybody to **lick his boots**. That's why nobody likes him.

  老闆要我們所有人都低聲下氣，難怪沒人喜歡他。

- **line one's own pocket**：to make money for oneself ina dishonest way 中飽私囊，自肥

  The local politician was **lining his own pocket** and did not win another election.

  地方政客因中飽私囊而落選。

- **lose one's shirt**：to lose all or most of one's money 輸光

  The man **lost his shirt** and now he is in serious financial situation.

  這人輸得精光，現在他的財務出了嚴重問題。

- **made to measure**：clothing that is made especially to fit the measurement of someone 量身訂製

  When I was working in Hong Kong I purchased several suits that were **made to measure**.

  當我在香港工作時訂製了幾套西裝。

佛要金裝人要衣裝 (Clothes Idioms)

- **make (something) by hand**：to make something with one's hand rather than with a machine 手工製作

  The woman likes to buy clothes that are **made by hand**.

  這女人喜歡買手工製作的衣服。

- **off-the-cuff/ speak off the cuff**：without preparation 臨時的，隨便的；在人前即席演講

  Our boss made a great **off-the-cuff** speech at the party last night.

  我們老闆昨晚即席的演講很精彩。

- **off the rack**：available for immediate purchase, ready-made 現成的

  The man always buys his suits **off the rack**.

  這人喜歡買現成的西裝。

- **old hat**：not new or different, old-fashioned 老式的，過時的

  We have been using the new computer program for many years. It is **old hat** now.

  我們已經用這個新電腦程式好多年；它現在已經落伍了。

- **on a shorstring**：on a very low budget, with very little money 小本經營，花很少錢

  We went to Europe **on a shoestring** and we enjoyed it very much.

  我們花很少錢去歐洲但我們覺得很喜歡。

佛要金裝人要衣裝 (Clothes Idioms)

- **on (someone's) coat-tails**：as a result of someone else doing something 蕭規曹隨

  The woman was elected to city council **on** her husband's **coat-tails**.

  這女子步她先生的後塵進入市議會。

- **out of fashion [style]**：not fashionable 落伍

  Most of the woman's clothes are **out of fashion**.

  這女子大部分的衣服都不流行了。

- **out of pocket**：the direct expense that one spends for business or personal use 自己掏腰包

  The money that I spent on my business trip was all **out of pocket**.

  這趟出差我都是自己掏腰包。

- **pass the hat**：to attempt to collect money from a group or people for some project or special cause 募捐

  We **passed the hat** in order to raise money to buy a movie project.

  我們為了要買部電影放映機而募款。

- **play one's cards close to one's chest**：to be extremely secretive and cautious about something 小心翼翼

  My boss always **plays his cards close to his chest** when he is negotiating with another company.

  我老闆在和其他公司磋商時總是小心翼翼。

O

佛要金裝人要衣裝 (Clothes Idioms)

pull oneself up by one's bootstraps：to improve oneself or achieve something through one's own effort 自立自強

> The boy **pulled himself up by his bootstraps** and went back and finished the university.
>
> 這男孩自立自強並回學校完成大學學業。

pull (something) out of a hat：to produce something as if by magic; to invent something 無中生有

> The lawyer said that she did not have information but suddenly she **pulled** it **out of a hat**.
>
> 律師先說她沒資料，但又突然憑空拿出來。

pull up one's socks：to make a great effort than before to do something 鼓起勁

> It is time that you **pull up your socks** and begin to work hard and take the job seriously.
>
> 該是你鼓起勁好好做事的時候了。

put on one's thinking cap：to think hard and long about something 仔細考慮

> I will **put on my thinking cap** and try to come up with a solution to the problem by next week.
>
> 我要仔細考慮並在下週前想出對這問題的解決之道。

put on the dog：to dress or entertain in an extravagant manner 耍派頭裝闊

> The couple **put on the dog** for the visit of their old college friend.
>
> 這對夫婦為了來訪的大學老友而擺闊。

佛要金裝人要衣裝 (Clothes Idioms)

- **put on one's clothes in mothballs**：to put something in storage with mothballs 收起來（mathball：樟腦丸）

    The woman plans to **put her coat in mothballs** for the winter.

    這女子計畫在冬天前先把大衣收起來。

- **quake [shake] in one's boots**：to be afraid, to shake from fear 擔心害怕

    I was **quaking in my boots** when my boss told me to come to his office.

    當老闆要我去他辦公室時，我有點擔心害怕。

- **ride on (someone's) coattails**：to have one's fortune or success depend on an-other person 繼承餘蔭

    My boss was **riding on the coattails** of his father and hoped to achieve success.

    我老闆繼承他父親的餘蔭希望能成功。

- **scare the pants off (someone)**：to frighten someone very badly 讓人驚惶害怕

    The big dog **scared the pants off** the little boy.

    這隻大狗嚇壞了小孩。

- **shoe is on the other foot**：the opposite is true, places are changed 風水輪流轉

    For a long time my friend laughed at my problem at work. Now, the **shoe is on the other foot** and he also has serious problems.

    多少年來我朋友總是因我在工作上有麻煩而笑我。風水輪流轉，現在他在工作上可是麻煩不少。

S

佛要金裝人要衣裝 (Clothes Idioms)

- **smarty pants**：a person who is annoying because he always has an answer or seem to know everything 自作聰明、自以為是的人

  > The boy is a **smarty pants**; he acts as if he knew everything.
  >
  > 這男孩自以為是，他自以為自己什麼都知道。

- **step into (someone's) shoe**：to take over a job or other role from someone 代理

  > I will have to **step into** my supervisor's **shoe** while he is away on vacation.
  >
  > 我必須在我主管度假時代理他。

- **stuffed shirt**：a person who is too rigid or too formal 道貌岸然的人

  > I do not want to invite my neighbor to come with us because he is a **stuffed shirt** and not very interesting to spend time with.
  >
  > 我不想邀請我鄰居一起來，因為他是個道貌岸然、無趣的人。

- **take one's hat off to (someone)**：to admire or respect or praise someone 羨慕，景仰或讚美某人

  > You have to **take your hat off to** my neighbor; he started a small business now it is very successful.
  >
  > 你必須向我鄰居致意；他以小生意開始的店現在已經非常成功。

- **talk through one's hat**：to say something without knowing or understanding the facts 信口開河

  > Our supervisor is **talking through his hat** and does not know what he is talking about.
  >
  > 我們的主管信口開河連自己說什麼都不知道。

S

佛要金裝人要衣裝 (Clothes Idioms)

- **throw [toss] one's hat into the ring**：to announce that one is running for an elected office 宣告參選

  The mayor **threw his hat into the ring** and decided to run for national office.

  市長宣布競選全國性公職。

- **tighten one's belt**：to live on less money than usual 縮衣節食

  If we want to go on a holiday to Europe this year, we will have to **tighten our bels** and begin to save some money.

  如果今年我們要去歐洲度假，我們就得縮衣節食，開始存點錢。

- **too big for one's boots [breeches]**：to think that you are more important than you really are 自大，膨風過度

  Our manager is **too big for his boots** and needs someone to make him realize that he is not so important.

  我們經理膨風過度，需要有人告訴他他並沒有那麼重要。

- **under one's belt**：in one's experience or possession, gained by effort and skill 有過的經驗 [歷練]

  Now that I have some job experience **under my belt** I will have more chances to apply for a good job.

  既然我已有過一些工作經驗，我該有更多的機會找個好工作。

T

佛要金裝人要衣裝 (Clothes Idioms)

wait for the other shoe to drop：to wait for something bad to happen, to wait for something to happen after alreay knowing that something is going to happen 等待必然會發生的（壞）事

> Our company announced that many people would lose their jobs. We are **waiting for the other shoe to drop** in order to learn more details of this announcement.
>
> 我們公司宣布很多人會沒工作。我們在等更多和這公告相關的細節以便進一步了解。

wash-and-wear：clothing that you can wash and it does not need to be ironed before you wear it 免燙的

> My uncle always like to buy **wash-and-wear** clothes.
>
> 我叔叔總是喜歡買免燙的衣服。

wear more than one hat/wear several hats：to have more than one set of responsibilities 身兼數職

> Our teacher **wears more than one hat**; she is the head of the school board as well as the coach of the swim team.
>
> 我們老師身兼數職，她是學校委員也是游泳隊教練。

wear the pants in one's family：to be the boss of a family or household 一家之主

> The woman **wears the pants in her family** and she is always telling her husband what to do.
>
> 這女人是一家之主，她總是告訴她先生做什麼。

佛要金裝人要衣裝 (Clothes Idioms)

- **with hat in hand**：with humanity 畢恭畢敬的

  The man came to his boss **with hat in hand** to ask for a raise in pay.

  這人畢恭畢敬地要求老闆加薪。

- **wolf in sheep's clothing**：a person who pretends to be good but is really bad 偽善者

  The man is a **wolf in sheep's clothing** and someone that you should be very careful around.

  這人是個偽善者，你可千萬要小心。

- **you bet your boots**：most certainly, yes indeed, absolutely 當然是，一定會…

  You bet your boots that I am going to apply for my passport as early as possible."

  我一定會盡早申請護照。

測驗題 (Idiom Quizzes)

Choose an idiom to replace the expression in the blankets:

1. The boy always comes to help his friends (very promptly) which is why everybody likes him.

   A dressed to kill   B below the belt   C under his belt   D at the drop of a hat

2. It is time that we (make a big effort) and try to get this job done.

   A fill our shoes   B keep our shirt on   C buckle down   D tighten our belts

3. The train was (full and very crowded) this morning.

   A off-the-cuff   B bursting at the seams   C decked outt   D flying by the seat of its pants

4. The woman was (dressed) in her best clothes when I saw her at theater last night.

   A decked out   B coming into fashion   C filling her shoes   D on a shoe-string

5. The fact that my friend is the new class president is (something that he should be proud of).

   A on his coattails   B a feather in his cap   C talking through his hat
   D up his sleeve

6. Our boss always (shows his feeling openly) and everyone knows his problems.

> A wears his heart on his sleeve   B wears the pants in his family   C pulls up his socks   D loses his shirt

7. Now that I have job experience (in my possessions) I will be able to look for a better job.

> A below the belt   B bruning in my pocket   C up my sleeve   D under my belt

8. The man is a (very formnal person) and nobody likes to invite him to a party.

> A wolf in sheep's clothing   B fine-tooth comb   C stuffed shirt   D been in his bonnet

9. The student will have to (make a greater effort) if he wants to pass his exam.

> A pull up his socks   B air dirty linen in public   C handle himself with kid gloves   D put on his thinking cap

10. You should try to (calm down). It is not good to become angry.

> A roll up your sleeve   B wear your heart on your sleeve   C lose your shirt   D keep your shirt on

11. The new supervisor has a reputation for being very mean so you will have to (treat her very gently).

> A fly by the seat of your pants   B handle her with kid gloves   C fit like a glove   D fill her shoes

12. It will be very difficult to (take his place) as he is one of the best worker in our company.

> A die with his boots on   B keep it under his hat   C fill his shoe   D pull up his socks

13. I don't want anyone to know when I will change jobs so could you please (keep it secret).

> A keep it under you hat   B roll up your sleeves   C put the shoe on the other foot   D keep your shirt on

14. My friend used to complain about having no money but now (the opposite is true) and it is me who has no money.

> A if the shoe fits wear it   B you bet your boots   C the shoe is on the other foort   D at the drop of a hat

15. You really have to (respect the man). He always works hard and never missed a day of work.

> A handle the man with kid gloves   B burn a hole in the man's pocket   C talk through the man's hat   D take your hat off to the man

測驗題 (Idiom Quizzes)

國家圖書館出版品預行編目資料

即選即用商務英文成語慣用語 / 李普生著. -- 初
版. -- 臺北市：五南, 2012.10

面；　公分

ISBN 978-957-11-6838-8（平裝）

1. 商業英文　2. 慣用語

805.123　　　　　　　　　　　　101017006

1AG1

即選即用商務英文成語慣用語

作　　　者	李普生
發 行 人	楊榮川
總 編 輯	王翠華
文字編輯	溫小瑩
版型設計	吳佳臻
封面設計	吳佳臻

出 版 者　五南圖書出版股份有限公司

地　　址：台北市大安區 106 和平東路二段 339 號 4 樓
電　　話：(02)2705-5066　傳　　真：(02)2706-6100
網　　址：http://www.wunan.com.tw
電子郵件：wunan@wunan.com.tw
劃撥帳號：01068953
戶　　名：五南圖書出版股份有限公司

法律顧問　元貞聯合法律事務所　張澤平律師

出版日期　2012 年 10 月　初版一刷

定　　價　280 元整